PAPER
WINDOWS

An Anthology of

Short Short

Stories

Compiling editor

Richard Baines

HODDER EDUCATION
A division of Hodder Headline Australia

Hodder Education
A Division of Hodder Headline Australia
(a member of the Hodder Headline Group)
10-16 South St
Rydalmere NSW 2116

First published by
Edward Arnold Australia in 1994
© Richard Baines 1994
Reprinted by Hodder Education in 1995, 1996, 1997, 1998 (twice)

National Library of Australia
Cataloguing-in-publication data

Paper Windows

ISBN 0 340 59379 2

1. Short stories, English. I. Baines, Richard.

823.0108

Text design by Nice Stuff
Illustrations by Melissa Webb
Typeset in 12/13 Garamond using Quark Xpress
Printed in Australia by Southwood Press

To Colleen, with love

A book is a paper house that one enters at one's own risk.

Gilroy Fisher

One of the neighborhood children had heard an insect sing on this slope one night. Buying a red lantern, he had come back the next night to find the insect. The night after that, there was another child. This new child could not buy a lantern. Cutting out the back and front of a small carton and papering it, he placed a candle on the bottom and fastened a string to the top. The number of children grew to five, and then to seven. They learned how to colour the paper that they stretched over the windows of the cutout cartons, and to draw pictures on it.

Yasunari Kawabata, *The Grasshopper and the Bell Cricket*

Contents

Preface

Wander through a bookstore. Find your way past the New Releases and the boxes of glossy paperbacks by popular authors, and look up. There are the book categories. Some are posted above the shelves in large type, some flicker in neon.

The lady with the blue rinse heads for the shelf marked CRIME; the parish priest edges towards the HORROR section. Over in TEENAGE, a mother tries to find something to occupy her daughter; the daughter herself is more interested in LIBIDO.

LIBIDO? Believe me. I've seen it.

(And how about TEENAGE? Teenage what? Teenage drama, teenage issues, teenage concerns? We are not told. I do not propose to enlighten you either.)

This book offers some of these choices. Many of the traditional categories are here: WAR, FANTASY, GHOSTS … Categories like these tend to be fairly arbitrary. One piece might well sit happily under two headings. 'Once in Love with Carla' is ROMANCE, but it could just as well have been labelled HUMOUR. Generally, the headings do help in identifying different literary genres but chiefly they focus on the varied and varying aspects of the human condition.

Paper Windows is a companion volume to *Paper Families*.

This is not a collection of short stories. It is a collection of short short stories. A short short story can be read in twelve minutes. It is strong and precise, tough as a nut and as single-minded. It has a high polish. Here we are closer to the poem than the novel.

A hundred and more years ago, before the days of fast foods and full engagement diaries, stories ran to many hundreds of pages. The novel reflected the pace of life and the architecture of the times. We came to associate good literature with heavy books. Today, things are changing. Our lives are in some ways more concentrated than they were then. We drive around in cars instead of striding off across the countryside. We live in apartment blocks twenty stories high rather than on sprawling properties. Perhaps these sleek and efficient stories, with their explosive moments of drama, humour and revelation, are a fitting shape for our modern way of life.

A short short story is easily accessible. These are bite-sized, lesson-sized stories. This book is for students from Year 9 and upwards. Each section of the book contains three stories; these are followed by *discussion* questions which may be used as written exercises or discussed by students in pairs or groups. Next, comes a selection of imaginative *activities* of varying lengths; the purpose of these is to help students think laterally and develop their creative writing skills.

Generally speaking, students do not write short stories. They write short short stories. It is appropriate, then, to discover just what can be done in such a short space. And how.

A selection of alternative approaches to the use of this material can be found in the appendices at the end of the book. On the other hand, these exercises may be happily ignored and the stories read purely for pleasure!

Richard Baines
April 1993

A Teacher's
Rewards

Robert Phillips

Robert Phillips was born in America. He is an award-winning poet, a prolific writer of short stories, who has also written anthologies and biographies.

'What'd you say your name was?' the old lady asked through the screen door. He stood on the dark porch.

'Raybe. Raybe Simpson. You taught me in the third grade, remember?'

'Simpson ... Simpson. Yes, I suppose so,' she said. Her hand remained on the latch.

'Of course you do. I was the boy with white hair. "Old Whitehead", my grandfather used to call me, though you wouldn't know that. I sat in the front row. You used to rap my knuckles with your ruler, remember?'

'Oh, I rapped a lot of knuckles in my time. Boys will be boys. Still, the white hair, the front row ...' Her voice trailed off as she made an almost audible effort to engage the ancient machinery of her memory.

'Sure you remember,' he said. '"Miss Scofield never forgets a name." That's what all the older kids told us. That's what all the other teachers said. "Miss Scofield never forgets a name."'

'Of course she doesn't. I never forgot a pupil's name in forty-eight years of teaching. Come right in.' She unlatched the screen door and swung it wide. The spring creaked.

'I can't stay long. I was in town for the day and thought I'd look you up. You were such a good teacher. I've never forgotten what you did for me.'

'Well, now, I consider that right kindly of you.' She looked him up and down through wire-rimmed spectacles. 'Just when was it I taught you?'

'Nineteen thirty-eight. Out to the old school.'

'Ah, yes. The old school. A pity about that fire.'

'I heard something about it burning down. But I've been away. When was that fire?'

'Oh, years ago. A year or two before I retired. After that I couldn't teach in the new brick schoolhouse they built. Something about the place. Too cold, too bright. And the classroom was so long. A body couldn't hardly see from the one end of it to the other …' She made a helpless gesture with her hand. He watched the hand in its motion: tiny, fragile, transparent, a network of blue veins running clearly beneath the surface; the skin hung in wrinkles like wet crepe paper. Denison paper, it had been called, when he was in school.

'That's rough. But you must have been about ready to retire anyhow, weren't you?'

Her watery blue eyes snapped. 'I should say not! All my life I've had a real calling for teaching. A real calling. I always said I would teach until I dropped in my tracks. It's such a rewarding field. A teacher gets her reward in something other than money … It was just that new red-brick schoolhouse! The lights were too bright, new-fangled fluorescent lights, bright yellow. And the room was too long …' Her gaze dared him to contradict her.

'I don't think much of these modern buildings, either.'

'Boxes,' she said firmly.

'Come again?'

'Boxes, boxes, nothing but boxes, that's all they are. I don't know what we're coming to, I declare. Well, now, Mr. —'

'Simpson. Mr. Simpson. But you can call me Raybe, like you always did.'

'Yes. Raybe. That's a nice name. Somehow it has an *honest* sound. Really, the things people name their children *these* days! There's one family named their children Cindy, Heidi and Dawn. They sound like creatures out of Walt Disney. The last year I taught, I had a student named Crystal. A little girl named Crystal! Why not name her Silverware, or China? And a boy named Jet. That was his first name, Jet. Or was it Astronaut? I don't know. Whatever it was it was terrible.'

'You once called me Baby-Raybe, and it caught on. That's what all the kids called me after that.'

'Did I? Oh, dear. Well, you must have done something babyish at the time.'

A shaft of silence fell between them. At last she smiled, as if to her-self, and said cheerily, 'I was just fixing to have some tea before you hap-pened by. Would you like some nice hot tea?'

'Well, I wasn't fixing to stay long, like I said.' He shuffled his feet.

'It'll only take a second. The kettle's been on all this time.' She seemed to have her heart set, and he was not one to disappoint. 'Okay, if you're having some.'

'Good. Do you take lemon or cream?'

'Neither. Actually I don't drink much tea. I'll just try it plain. With sugar. I've got a sweet tooth.'

'A sweet tooth! Let me see. Is that one of the things I remember about you? Raybe Simpson, a sweet tooth? No, I don't think so. One of the boys always used to eat Baby Ruth candy bars right in class. The minute my back was turned he'd sneak another Baby Ruth out of his desk. But that wasn't you, was it?'

'No.'

'I didn't think it was you,' she said quickly. 'I called it the blackboard. Did you know, in that new school building, it was green?'

'What was green?'

'The blackboard was *green*. And the chalk was *yellow*. Something about it being easier on the children's eyes. And they had the nerve to call them blackboards, too, mind you. How do you expect children to learn if you call what's green, black?'

'Hmmm.'

She was getting down two dainty cups with pink roses painted on them. She put them on a tin tray and placed a sugar bowl between them. The bowl was cracked down the middle and had been taped with Scotch tape, which had yellowed. When the tea finally was ready, they adjourned to the living room. The parlor, she called it.

'Well, how've you been, Miss Scofield?' he asked.

'Can't complain, except for a little arthritis in my hands. Can't com-plain.'

'Good.' He studied her hands, then glanced around. 'Nice little place you got here.' He took a sip of the tea, found it strong and bitter, added two more heaping spoons of sugar.

'Well, it's small, of course, but it serves me. It serves me.' She settled back in her rocker.

'You still Miss Scofield?'

'How's that?' She leaned forward on her chair, as if to position her ear closer to the source.

'I asked you, your name is still Miss Scofield? You never got married?'

'Mercy no. I've always been an unclaimed blessing. That's what I've always called myself. "An unclaimed blessing." ' She smiled sweetly.

'You still live alone, I take it.'

'Yes indeed. I did once have a cat. A greedy old alley cat named Tom. But he died. Overeating did it, I think. Ate me out of house and home, pretty near.'

'You don't say.'

'Oh, yes indeed. He'd eat anything. Belly got big as a basketball, nearabout. He was good company, though. Sometimes I miss that old Tom.'

'I should think so.'

An old-fashioned clock chimed overhead.

'What business did you say you were in, Mr. Simp … Raybe?'

'Didn't say.'

'That's right, you didn't say. Well, just what is it?'

'Right now I'm unemployed.'

She set her teacup upon a lace doily on the tabletop and made a little face of disapproval. 'Unemployed. I see. Then how do you get along?'

'Oh, I manage, one way or the other. I've been pretty well taken care of these last ten years. I been away.'

'You're living with your folks? Is that it?' Encouragement bloomed on her cheeks.

'My folks are dead. They were dead when I was your student, if you'll remember. Grandfather died too. I lived with an aunt. She's dead now.'

'Oh, I'm sorry. I don't think I realized at the time — '

'No, I don't think you did … That's all right, Miss Scofield. You had a lot of students to look after.'

'Yes, but still and all, it's unlike me not to have remembered or known that one of my boys was an *orphan*. You don't mind if I use that word, do you, Mr … Raybe? Lots of people are sensitive about words.'

'I don't mind. I'm not sensitive.'

'No, I should think not. You're certainly a big boy, now. And what happened to all that hair? Why, you're bald as a baby.' Looking at his head, she laughed a laugh as scattered as buckshot. 'My, you must be hot in that jacket. Why don't you take it off? It looks very heavy.'

'I'll keep it on, if you don't mind.'

'Don't mind a bit, so long's you're comfortable.' What did he have in that jacket, she wondered. He was carrying something in there.

'I'm just fine,' he said, patting the jacket.

She began to rock in her chair and looked around the meager room to check its presentability to unexpected company. Maybe he had his dinner in there, in a paper poke, and was too embarrassed to show it.

'Well, now, what do you remember about our year together that I may have forgotten? Were you in Jay McMaster's class? Jay was a lovely boy. So polite. You can always tell good breeding — '.

'He was a year or two ahead of me. You're getting close, though.'

'Well, of course I am. How about Nathan Pillsbury? The dentist's son. He was in your class, wasn't he?'

'That's right.'

'See!' She exclaimed triumphantly. 'Another lovely boy. His parents had a swimming pool. One Christmas Nathan brought me an enormous poinsettia plant. It filled the room, nearly.'

'He was in my class, all right. He was the teacher's pet, you might say.' Raybe observed her over the rim of his bitter cup. He looked at her knuckles.

'Nathan, my pet? Nathan Pillsbury? I don't remember any such thing. Besides, I never played favorites. That's a bad practice.' She worked her lips to and fro.

'So's rapping people's knuckles,' he laughed, putting his half-full cup on the floor.

She laughed her scattered little laugh again. 'Oh, come now, Raybe. Surely it was deserved, if indeed I ever did rap your knuckles.'

'You rapped them, all right,' he said soberly.

'Did I? Did I really? Yes, I suppose I did. What was it for, do you remember? Passing notes? Gawking out the window?'

'Wasn't for any one thing. You did it lots of times. *Dozens* of times.' He cleared his throat.

'Did I? Mercy me. It doesn't seem to me that I did. I only rapped knuckles upon extreme provocation, you know. *Extreme* provocation.' She took a healthy swallow of tea. What was it she especially remembered about this boy? Something. It nagged at her. She couldn't remember what it was. Some trait of personality.

'You did it lots of times,' he continued. 'In front of the whole class. They laughed at me.'

'I did? Goodness, what a memory! Well, it doesn't seem to have done you any harm. A little discipline never hurt anybody ... What was it you said you've been doing professionally?'

'I been in prison,' he said with a pale smile. He watched her mouth draw downward.

'Prison? You've been in *prison*? Oh, I see, it's a joke.' She tried to laugh again, but this time the little outburst wouldn't scatter.

'*You* try staying behind those walls for ten years and see if you think it's a joke.' He fumbled in his pocket for a pack of cigarettes, withdrew a smoke and slowly lit it. He blew a smoke ring across the table.

'Well, I must say! You're certainly the only boy I ever had that ... that ended up in prison! But I'm sure there were ... *circumstances* ... leading up to that. I'm sure you're a fine lad, through it all.' She worked her lips faster now. Her gaze traveled to the window that looked out upon the night.

'Yeah, there were *circumstances,* as you call it. Very special circum-stances.' He blew an enormous smoke ring her way. The old woman began to cough. 'It's the smoke. I'm not used to people smoking around me. Do you mind refraining?'

'Yeah, I do mind,' he said roughly. 'I'm going to finish this cigarette, no matter what.'

'Well, if you must, you must,' she said nervously, half-rising. 'But let me just open that window a little — '

'SIT BACK DOWN IN THAT CHAIR!'

She fell back into the rocker.

'Now, you listen to me, you old bitch,' he began.

'Don't call me names. Don't you dare! How *dare* you? No wonder you were behind bars. A common jailbird. A degenerate. No respect for your elders.'

'Shut up, grandma.' He tossed the cigarette butt to the floor and ground it out on what looked like an Oriental rug. Her eyes bulged.

'I remember you very clearly, now,' she exclaimed, her hands to her brow. 'I remember you! You were no good to start with. No motivation. No follow through. I knew just where you'd end up. You've run true to form.' Her gaze was defiant.

'Shut your mouth, bitch,' he said quietly, beginning at last to unzip his leather jacket.

'I will *not,* I'll have my say. You were a troublemaker, too. I remember the day you wrote nasty, nasty words on the wall in the supply closet. Horrible words. And then when I went back to get papers to distribute, I saw those words. I had to read them, and I knew who wrote them, all right.'

'I didn't write them.'

'Oh, you wrote them, all right. And I whacked your knuckles good with a ruler, if I remember right.'

'You whacked my knuckles good, but I didn't write those words.'

'*Did!*'

'*Didn't.*' They sounded like a pair of school children. He squirmed out of the jacket.

'I never made mistakes of that kind,' she said softly, watching him shed the jacket. 'I knew just who needed strict discipline in my class.'

He stood before her now, holding the heavy jacket in his hand. Underneath he wore only a tee shirt of some rough gray linsey-woolsey material. She saw that his arms were heavily muscled, and he saw that she saw. She was positive she could smell the odor of the prison upon him, though the closest she had come to a prison was reading Dickens.

'I never made mistakes,' she repeated feebly. 'And now, you'd better put that coat right back on and leave. Go back to wherever you came from.'

'Can't do that just yet, bitch. I got a score to settle.'

'Score? To settle?' She placed her hands upon the rocker arms for support.

'Yeah. I had a long time to figure it all out. Ten years to figure it out. Lots of nights I'd lie there on that board of a bed in that puke-hole and I'd try to piece it all together. How I come to be *there*. Was it my aunt? Naw, she did the best she could without any money. Was it the fellas I took up with in high school? Naw, something happened before that, or I'd never have taken up with the likes of them in the first place, that rocky crowd. And then one night it came to me. *You* were the one.'

'Me? The one? The one for what?' Her lips worked furiously now, in and out like a bellows. Her hands tightly gripped the rocker's spindle arms.

'The one who sent me there. Because you *picked* on me all the time. Made me out worse than I was. You never gave me the chance the others had. The other kids left me out of things, because you were always saying I was bad. And you always told me I was dirty. Just because my aunt couldn't keep me in clean shirts like some of the others. You punished me for everything that happened. But the worst was the day of the words on the wall. You hit me so hard my knuckles bled. My hands were sore as boils for weeks.'

'*That's* an exaggeration.'

'No it isn't. They're *my* hands, I ought to know. And do you know who wrote those words on the closet wall? *Do you know?*' he screamed, putting his face right down next to hers.

'No, who?' she whispered, breathless with fright.

'*Nathan Pillsbury*, that's who!' he shouted, clenching his teeth and shaking her frail body within his grasp. '*Nathan Pillsbury, Nathan Pillsbury!*'

'Let me go,' she whimpered. 'Let me go.'

'I'll let you go after my score is settled.'

The old woman's eyes rolled toward the black, unseeing windows. 'What are you going to do to me?' she rasped.

'Just settle, lady,' he said, taking the hammer from his jacket. 'Now, put you hands on the tabletop.'

'My hands? On the tabletop?' she whispered.

'On the tabletop,' he repeated pedantically, a teacher. 'Like this.' He made two fists and placed them squarely on the surface.

She refused.

'*Like this!*' he yelled, wrenching her quivering hands and forcing them to the tabletop. Then with his free hand he raised the hammer.

For once, he finished something.

Birthday

Mary Roberts

Mary Roberts was born in England, but came to Australia as a child. Her family lived in South Tasmania by the sea, but, when she married, she moved to Victoria. She has three children, enjoys gardening, and continues to write stories.

The overnight bus was packed. Either there was no air conditioning or the driver had been told to conserve petrol, but each breath I took of the stuffy air — heavy with fumes of beer and cigarettes from the noisy gang in the back, made me increasingly nauseated. How humiliating if I had to grope for one of the lined paper bags in the back of the seat ahead. How I wished the fat man next to me, snoring steadily, didn't think my shoulder was his pillow as he slumped sideways.

The din of shouts and laughter from the back rose to a crescendo.

'Hey fellas! What about cutting it out and letting the others get a bit of shut eye?' the driver beseeched.

'Hear hear!' groaned a couple of weary voices.

'You keep your eye on the road, mate,' someone answered. 'We've paid our fares and we wanna relax. That right, chaps?'

'Yairs! Thass right, Shorty.'

I rubbed the steamy window beside me. Gum trees, bleached and dead looking in the glare of the headlights, flashed past. To my weary eyes some looked like menacing figures with weird faces. I counted the red eyes of the white road markers — one, two three, four ... There seemed to be a heavy weight inside me, making it so hard to breathe, pinning me to the sticky seat. If only I were home in my own bed, to sleep ...

A sudden lurch jerked me awake. Had the driver closed his eyes for a second? He was dragging on the wheel as he took a corner on the wrong side. There was a sudden explosive sense of danger — headlights blazing — the vast bulk of a semi-trailer, screeching brakes, the shuddering impact of a side swipe and we were crashing through a safety fence.

I can't describe the horror of the next seconds? minutes? eternity? the falling, crashing, bouncing, screaming, down, down, down! And pain! An agony that crumpled my body like a hand crushing a tissue paper ball! 'Oh, God!' I screamed …

I woke to my scream unable to credit I was in my own bed, that the terrifying experience was only a nightmare. My whole body, wet with sweat, was shaking and my pounding heart felt as if it would burst. I switched on the light. 1.35 a.m. Hey, it was Tuesday 9 May, my birthday. I was thirteen. What a start to the day, I thought. How would I go to sleep now?

'I had THE most awful nightmare last night,' I announced at breakfast after I'd opened my cards and presents.

'What did you have for supper, Kate?' my step-mother asked.

'Only the usual,' I said. 'No, it wasn't last night — it was early this morning because I looked at my watch and it was 1.35.'

'Bad enough to wake you up, was it?' asked Dad.

'I've never had such a vivid dream — never,' I insisted. 'It was horrible.' As I spoke the memory surged back strongly and I found it hard to tell it all. Then I noticed Dad's face. It was white and his eyes were full of angry pain.

'Who's been talking to you?' he demanded.

'Talking to me? What d'you mean? Talking about what?'

Dad turned accusingly to my step-mother. 'Sheila?'

'Don't be stupid, David. No! Why should I?'

Dad sighed. 'Sorry, love. No, of course you wouldn't. Forgive me.' He leant forward and grasped my hand. 'Kate, you've shaken me up, I don't mind telling you. But you're thirteen now — a teenager — old enough to grapple with the big things in life. You know your mother died when you were a baby?'

'Yes, of course I know. You told me yourself and Granny's told me too. She said my Mum died in a car accident, but you weren't driving or anything.'

'That's right,' Dad said. 'That's all we wanted you to know. But here's why you've given me such a shock. What you've described is actually what happened. The passenger bus she was on hit a semi-trailer and crashed down a steep gully just after midnight. It was a dreadful accident — ten killed and lots of serious injuries.'

'And my Mum?'

'When the rescue party found her, you'd just been born, but she died when they tried to put her on a stretcher. I can't understand how you could have experienced the crash,' Dad said slowly.

What was there to say? The three of us sat in silence. A big WHY? nagged me.

You've got to believe me when I tell you I had exactly the same experience a year later. Every detail was the same — the atmosphere, the passengers, the talk, the dreadful horror. Again I woke screaming. And again it was 1.35 a.m. It was my fourteenth birthday.

This time I deliberately kept quiet and didn't tell a soul. But I couldn't forget.

The night before my fifteenth birthday, I was really scared. I dreaded the hours ahead. I hung around with Dad and Sheila until they went to bed. I had a nagging fear that maybe the third time I had the nightmare, I mightn't wake up. I might die too. It sounds morbid but the reality of those dreams was so powerful.

I made up my mind to stay up all night: to keep the light on and read: walk the floor if needs be. Never mind if I was zonked next day. I couldn't trust myself to read in bed in case I dozed off. I took a blanket and curled up for warmth in an old armchair by the slightly open window. I'd two good library books to read. I began the first book and was soon deep into it ...

The bus droned on. Gum trees loomed up in the ghostly shapes and fled behind us. Passengers slumped uncomfortably in their seats grunted, sighed, turned.

'Hey, fellas! What about cutting it out and letting the others get a bit of shut eye?' asked the driver amiably.

Suddenly he was wrenching the bus around a bend, lights glared; there was a splintering crash; shouts and screams and we were lurching, toppling, turning and crashing, down, down, down. I was squeezed in what seemed like a dark tunnel, a tunnel pressing me tightly. I must escape! Help me! Push me ... push me ... I was free! Around me was a murky darkness, a blinding moving light, noise, confusion.

I heard an angry, despairing wail — the voice of a new born baby.

The voice was mine.

The Fly

Arthur Porges

Arthur Porges was a mathematician who taught at several universities in America until he retired in 1975. His best writing was in the areas of science fiction, fantasy and horror, and throughout the 1950s and 1960s, his writing appeared in magazines, particularly *The Magazine of Fantasy and Science Fiction.*

Shortly after noon the man unslung his Geiger counter and placed it carefully upon a flat rock by a thick, inviting patch of grass. He listened to the faint, erratic background ticking for a moment, then snapped off the current. No point in running the battery down just to hear stray cosmic rays and residual radioactivity. So far he'd found nothing potent, not a single trace of workable ore.

Squatting, he unpacked an ample lunch of hard-boiled eggs, bread, fruit, and a thermos of black coffee. He ate hungrily, but with the neat, crumbless manners of an outdoorsman; and when the last bite was gone, he stretched out, braced on his elbows, to sip the remaining drops of coffee. It felt mighty good, he thought, to get off your feet after a six-hour hike through rough country.

As he lay there, savoring the strong brew, his gaze suddenly narrowed and became fixed. Right before his eyes, artfully spun between two twigs and a small, mossy boulder, a cunning snare for the unwary spread its threads of wet silver in the network of death. It was the instinctive creation of a master engineer, a nearly perfect logarithmic spiral, stirring gently in a slight updraft.

He studied it curiously, tracing with growing interest the special cable, attached only at the ends, that led from a silk cushion at the web's center up to a crevice in the boulder. He knew that the mistress of this snare must be hidden there, crouching with one hind foot on her primitive telegraph wire and awaiting those welcome vibrations which meant a victim thrashing hopelessly among the sticky threads.

He turned his head and soon found her. Deep in the dark crevice the spider's eyes formed a sinister, jeweled pattern. Yes, she was at home, patiently watchful. It was all very efficient and, in a reflective mood, drowsy from his exertions and a full stomach, he pondered the small miracle before him: how a speck of protoplasm, a mere dot of white nerve tissue which was a spider's brain, had antedated the mind of Euclid by countless centuries. Spiders are an ancient race; ages before man wrought wonders through his subtle abstractions of points and lines, a spiral not to be distinguished from this one winnowed the breezes of some prehistoric summer.

Then he blinked, his attention once more sharpened. A glowing gem, glistening metallic blue, had planted itself squarely upon the web. As if manipulated by a conjurer, the bluebottle fly had appeared from nowhere. It was an exceptionally fine specimen, he decided, large, perfectly formed, and brilliantly rich in hue.

He eyed the insect wonderingly. Where was the usual panic, the frantic struggling, the shrill, terrified, buzzing? It rested there with an odd indifference to restraint that puzzled him.

There was at least one reasonable explanation. The fly might be sick or dying, the prey of parasites. Fungi and the ubiquitous roundworms shattered the ranks of even the most fertile. So unnaturally still was this fly that the spider, wholly unaware of its feathery landing, dreamed on in her shaded lair.

Then, as he watched, the bluebottle, stupidly perverse, gave a single sharp tug; its powerful wings blurred momentarily and a high-pitched buzz sounded. The man sighed, almost tempted to interfere. Not that it mattered how soon the fly betrayed itself. Eventually the spider would have made a routine inspection; and unlike most people, he knew her for a staunch friend of man, a tireless killer of insect pests. It was not for him to steal her dinner and tear her web.

But now, silent and swift, a pea on eight hairy, agile legs, she glided over her swaying net. An age-old tragedy was about to be enacted, and the man waited with pitying interest for the inevitable denouement.

About an inch from her prey, the spider paused briefly, estimating the situation with diamond-bright, soulless eyes. The man knew what would follow. Utterly contemptuous of a mere fly, however large, lacking either sting or fangs, the spider would unhesitatingly close in, swathe the insect with silk, and drag it to her nest in the rock, there to be drained at leisure.

But instead of a fearless attack, the spider edged cautiously nearer. She seemed doubtful, even uneasy. The fly's strange passivity apparently worried her. He saw the needle-pointed mandibles working, ludicrously suggestive of a woman wringing her hands in agonized indecision.

Reluctantly she crept forward. In a moment she would turn about, squirt a preliminary jet of silk over the bluebottle, and by dexterously rotating the fly with her hind legs, wrap it in a gleaming shroud.

And so it appeared, for satisfied with a closer inspection, she forgot her fears and whirled, thrusting her spinnerets towards the motionless insect.

Then the man saw a startling, an incredible thing. There was a metallic flash as a jointed, shining rod stabbed from the fly's head like some fantastic rapier. It licked out with lightning precision, pierced the spider's plump abdomen, and remained extended, forming a terrible link between them.

He gulped, tense with disbelief. A bluebottle fly, a mere lapper of carrion, with an extensible, sucking proboscis! It was impossible. Its tongue is only an absorbing cushion, designed for sponging up liquids. But then was this really a fly after all? Insects often mimic each other and he was no longer familiar with such points. No, a bluebottle is umistakable; besides, this was a true fly, two wings and everything. Rusty or not, he knew that much.

The spider had stiffened as the queer lance struck home. Now she was rigid, obviously paralyzed. And her swollen abdomen was contracting like a tiny fist as the fly sucked its juices through that slender, pulsating tube.

He peered more closely, raising himself to his knees and longing for a lens. It seemed to his straining gaze as if that gruesome beak came not from the mouth region at all, but through a minute, hatchlike opening between the faceted eyes, with a nearly invisible square door ajar. But that was absurd; it must be the glare, and — ah! Flickering, the rod retracted; there was definitely no such opening now. Apparently the bright sun was playing tricks. The spider stood shriveled, a pitiful husk, still upright on her thin legs.

One thing was certain, he must have this remarkable fly. If not a new species, it was surely very rare. Fortunately it was stuck fast in the web. Killing the spider could not help it. He knew the steely toughness of those elastic strands, each a tight helix filled with superbly tenacious gum. Very few insects, and those only among the strongest, ever tear free. He gingerly extended his thumb and forefinger. Easy now; he had to pull the fly loose without crushing it.

Then he stopped, almost touching the insect, and staring hard. He was uneasy, a little frightened. A brightly glowing spot, brilliant even in the glaring sunlight, was throbbing on the very tip of the blue abdomen. A reedy, barely audible whine was coming from the trapped insect. He thought momentarily of fireflies, only to dismiss the notion with scorn for his own stupidity. Of course, a firefly is actually a beetle, and this thing was — not that, anyway.

Excited, he reached forward again. But as his plucking fingers approached, the fly rose smoothly in a vertical ascent, lifting a pyramid of taut strands and tearing a gap in the web as easily as a falling stone. The man was alert, however. His cupped hand, nervously swift, snapped over the insect, and he gave a satisfied grunt.

But the captive buzzed in his eager grasp with a furious vitality that appalled him, and he yelped as a searing, slashing pain scalded the sensitive palm. Involuntarily he relaxed his grip. There was a streak of electric blue as his prize soared, glinting in the sun. For an instant he saw that odd glowworm taillight, a dazzling spark against the darker sky, then nothing.

He examined the wound, swearing bitterly. It was purple, and already little blisters were forming. There was no sign of a puncture. Evidently the creature had not used its lancet, but merely spurted venom — acid, perhaps — on the skin. Certainly the injury felt very much like a bad burn. Damn and blast! He'd kicked away a real find, an insect probably new to science. With a little more care he might have caught it.

Stiff and vexed, he got sullenly to his feet and repacked the lunch kit. He reached for the Geiger counter, snapped on the current, took one step towards a distant rocky outcrop — and froze. The slight background noise had given way to a veritable roar, an electronic avalanche that could mean only one thing. He stood there, scrutinizing the grassy knoll and shaking his head in profound mystification. Frowning, he put down the counter. As he withdrew his hand, the frantic chatter quickly faded out. He waited, half-stooped, a blank look in his eyes. Suddenly they lit with doubting, half-fearful comprehension. Catlike, he stalked the clicking instrument, holding one arm outstretched, gradually advancing the blistered palm.

And the Geiger counter raved anew.

A Teacher's Rewards   *Robert Phillips*

Discussion

1   Do you think Miss Scofield got what she deserved? Give reasons for your point of view.

2   What are some of the ideas about school life that the author is asking us to consider? Go into some detail in your discussion, and refer closely to the story.

3   A *motif* in literature is a recurring image or idea which runs through a piece of writing. The motif of 'hands' is present in this story.
    a   Read the story again, and make note of the importance that is given to hands from the start.
    b   Why do you think the author has done this? Does it add to the horror of the piece? Explain.

Activities

1   'For once, he finished something.' — The story ends there, but Miss Scofield's life may not. What do you think happened to her? Devise three possible endings to this short short story.

2   The story of the attack upon Miss Scofield breaks in the newspapers the following morning. Choose two papers, different in their outlook and approach, and write the article for each, showing how an incident can be interpreted in two very different ways.

3   There is much skill in taking an ordinary everyday scene, such as two people drinking tea together, and building up the tension and suspense until the story reaches a fever pitch of nightmare proportions.
    a   Make a note of the ways in which this is done in 'A Teacher's Rewards'. Raybe's past, and its significance, is slowly revealed. His language changes. There is a mystery about what is concealed in his jacket. And when the story is over, early lines, like: 'I've never forgotten what you did for me', take on an ominous overtone. Try this yourself.
    b   Take a seemingly ordinary situation and turn it — slowly — into something frightening. If you would like some ideas, here are three possible starting points.
      •   A cat brings home a dead bird ...
      •   Three female university students share a flat. One evening an old man, tired and bedraggled, turns up on the doorstep ...
      •   Peter, travelling to an important business meeting in the city, suddenly finds that he has left his wallet at home ...

Birthday *Mary Roberts*

Discussion

1 Why did Kate wake up screaming every year at 1.35 a.m. on 9 May?

2 In your own words, and clearly, re-tell the story of Kate's birth.

3 A technique that writers sometimes use is to echo at the end of a story a line which appeared somewhere near its beginning. This *linking of the two sections of a story* often proves very effective. What line is repeated in this story? What is the purpose of this repetition? Is it effective? Is there any other repetition (other than repetition of lines) in the story?

Activities

1 Re-tell your worst nightmare. How does it end?

2 Imagine that it is a year later in 'Birthday', and the date is 8 May. What happens to Kate that night? Write a page.

3 Write a short short story of your own about any subject you choose. The only rules are that the first sentence must be: 'The overnight bus was packed', and the final sentence must read: 'The voice was mine'.

The Fly *Arthur Porges*

Discussion

1 What did the fly do to the spider? What did the fly do to the man? What did the man 'half-fearfully comprehend' at the end of the piece?

2 Is 'The Fly' a horror story, and, if so, why? Should it not rather be listed under the heading of fantasy or science fiction? Discuss your point of view.

3 Read the descriptions of the spider, the spider's web, and the fight between the spider and fly. How much is a knowledge of science responsible for such descriptive passages? Talk about specific words and allusions in your answer.

Activities

1 You are allowed to add one more paragraph to the end of this story. What happens?

2   Imagine that you are the fly. Re-tell this story from your point of view, making it very clear what you think of the spider and the man.

3   Many films have used animals, birds and insects as a source of horror. The horror comes when these creatures act in unpredictable ways. For example, when maddened birds flock together to attack ordinary people (an idea first presented in a short story by Daphne du Maurier, and later as a film in *The Birds* by Alfred Hitchcock), the horror begins to build.

Horror and humour are first cousins. If we do not believe in the horror, if it does not convince us, then we tend to laugh. Some people go to horror movies for a good laugh. Explore this area yourself. Either write a genuine horror story centering round an animal (for example, a sloth), a bird (for example, an owl) or an insect (for example, a praying mantis), or try to make your readers laugh by writing a horror story. Be warned: this is harder than it sounds.

TEENAGE

Are You

Sarah Katherine Pidgeon

Sarah Katherine Pidgeon wrote 'Are You' when she was fifteen and still a student at Duval High School in Armidale. It was one of the best entries in the *Sydney Morning Herald* Young Writers' competition for that year. Although it is often recommended to students that they write about what they know, Sarah says, 'I've written about a subject so removed from my own experience'.

Caroline sat silently at the table, not eating, not listening, just sitting quite still. She started to rub her thumb rhythmically up and down the stem of her knife as it lay beside her plate, concentrating hard on the texture of the knife. It seemed important just then, if only because it might keep her calm. Her skin had that very tender, sensitive feel that it got whenever she was sick or upset, and with the skin of her thumb she imagined that she could feel every bump of the rose petals, every line of their stems, every scratch of the leaf veins, every detail which made up the delicate engraving on the knife's handle.

Her father spilt some wine, making her mother twitch irritably. She didn't say anything, the body language was enough. Her father mopped up the mess slowly and painstakingly, knowing just how this would annoy her mother. No one spoke. Caroline sat deeply in her chair, again seeking comfort from the small sensations she found all around her. She felt the cane of her chair penetrating the thin material of her school uniform, pricking the backs of her legs and her back. The tiny fibres pressing into her skin seemed like sharp needles, sending little shots of pain through her body.

Fixing her mind on her plate for the first time, she realised what trouble her mother had gone to in preparing this meal. She was surprised — lately it had just been TV dinners and tins of stuff, but tonight they were having a real gourmet dish. Through the door to the kitchen she glimpsed a moist, rich-looking chocolate cake cooling on a cake rack. Caroline had always loved chocolate cake, but suddenly she thought that she would never be able to stomach one again. Picking up her fork she started to play with the fancy sauce that had been dripped over the vegetables, but made no attempt at eating. Her mouth was dry, her throat felt tight; she knew that she would not be able to swallow.

Her parents seemed equally uninterested in the meal, eating slowly and methodically. They were both thinking about something serious, that was obvious, though they tried not to show it. Caroline was used to the silences by now, for whatever reason they occurred. The three of them never talked anymore, not like they used to. She could remember a time when they were always discussing things, laughing or sharing their feelings, but all that had changed in the past few months. Now any attempt at conversation petered out almost at once, or her parents would differ on some subject and bicker about it, making biting comments which seemed to hurt Caroline most of all.

Her thoughts switched to the beach holiday they had taken one year, when it had poured the whole darn week. The surprising thing was, instead of feeling miserable and annoyed, they were really happy. Tucked up nice and snug in their rented cabin, they'd sit and talk … talk about anything. Now she couldn't remember about what, just that they had never been so close. The three of them in the shabby surroundings, huddled around that wretched little one-bar heater, yet so warm and happy.

'At least eat the potato, dear,' her mother spoke gently, recalling her from her detached reflections. She was really trying tonight.

'She doesn't have to eat anything if she doesn't want to,' said her father. Her parents looked at each other then, a challenge in each other's eyes. Still they said nothing, but just stared, her mother tight-lipped and flashing-eyed, her father laid-back yet equally determined.

And then Caroline knew. It had been coming for weeks, the chill in the house becoming more painfully obvious every day, and yet she had fought it, rejecting the knowledge of it, refusing to accept it.

Until now. And now she had to face it. The time had come for her to stop hiding.

A pain which started in her chest and then spread throughout her body engulfed her. She seemed to stop breathing, but she mustn't have, because she remained quite conscious and alive to the pain, which was worse and more acute than any she had known before. Then, as suddenly as it had started, the pain subsided, leaving her numb, void of all feeling, oblivious to everything around her. And in this inert frame of mind she felt she could cope. It didn't really matter.

A loud clatter jolted Caroline out of her dazed state. Her fork had slipped from her loose hold and now lay on the polished floorboards.

The sound must have disturbed her parents, too, because they stopped staring at each other and were now looking at her.

Caroline retrieved her fork, and deliberately laid it aside, folding her hands in her lap. She knew that now it would come. She couldn't bring herself to look at either of her parents, so she stared instead at the table-cloth, taking in the delicate pattern of flowers that had been so lovingly embroidered onto it by some long-dead ancestor. The pattern was complicated and beautiful, each stitch perfectly and strategically placed. It was really a fascinating piece of work; funny how she had never noticed that before.

Finally her mother spoke. 'Darling, your father and I have come to a very ... important, and difficult decision —'

Here Caroline interrupted her. She couldn't stand it. Better to get it out quickly.

'I know. I know. You don't have to tell me.' Speaking was an effort, but somehow she got it out. Her parents were looking apprehensive now. She took a deep breath, choking back the tears that were stinging her eyes. 'You're getting a divorce.' Saying it seemed to make a terrible confirmation of the fact, and yet her question was almost a plea. ' — Aren't you?'

The Toy Girl

Paula Clark

The grass was wet against her face and smeared her as she looked up. Irregular shifting shapes surrounded her in the darkness and laughter grew from one side and shimmered over her head. One of the shapes reached out and touched her shoulder — 'Paula?'

The voice, incredibly loud, ricocheted inside her head. She winced and squinted to focus on the blank face, dissolving into helpless, wheezy giggles when the shape became Helen, her eyes wide and amazed.

Arms lifted her (or pulled her down) and half carried her, mumbling and weak, across the damp park. She could hear voices swirling through the vapour in her mind, some familiar, some not, some from outside, some from within. 'Drunk? She's blasted! What was she doing?'

Her kitchen appeared from somewhere and she was sat down, blinking in the hard electric light. She looked absently at her hands. They were bruised with the cold but she felt nothing and the uncomprehending giggling bubbled uncontrollably out of her.

The house seemed full of people. Their voices and movements blurred around her and vaguely she heard the cupboard doors open and hungry hands reach inside and take. The words asking them not to formed in her mind but diffused into confused sobbing and mumbling before they reached her mouth. She could hear pop music from somewhere and a muffled fear turned in her stomach, but then the light began to dim around the edges and the sound to spin away and darkness flowed over the room.

The wrenching inside her own head woke her up. Aware of a throbbing silence and, strangely, the heavy smell of paint in the room, she ached her eyes open and blinked painfully around her. The image which faced her made her recoil in horror, taking a sudden, frightened breath. The walls ... oh my God the walls ... paint ... Random sprayed lines dribbled across them, coating the ripped wallpaper as it hung like jagged leaves around her. The pounding in her head grew and her stomach tumbled as she saw the room completely now, smashed and littered, a red wine stain seeping like blood in the corner of the carpet. She sat up, spinning, trembling, her mouth horribly dry as fear burned in her throat. She walked almost dreamlike through the house as though it were some weird, undiscovered cave. It was totally unfamiliar, a sickening mixture of garish, hateful colour and destruction.

What had they done? She stared disbelievingly around her, a cold numbness spreading inside her and beginning to squeeze hot tears down her face. The sweet, gluish smell of vomit grew in the hallway and as she heard the crunch of her parents' car in the drive she stood, uncertain, caught between the two. As the key scraped in the lock, the discarded Toy Girl wiped her eyes and, reaching down, gently picked up a torn piece of paper from the floor. She curled herself up in the corner by the stairs and pressed her face into her knees, her trembling hands tightly clutching the tiny fragment of a birthday card.

East Wind

Gillian Dawson

Gillian Dawson lives on a smallholding in the Huon Valley of Tasmania, where she raises chickens, children and vegetables, and writes poetry and short stories.

When autumn comes, we pick almonds from the ragged tree over the fence. And Granny Smiths, polished by the east wind. The valley fog closes our throats, and we hear the black swans calling across the river, like lost children.

I remember the night we thought we had lost him: Michael was three then, and the pink and blue neon lights scattered off his excited eyes as he ran ahead of us. And our desperate searching through the dark park and the alien city eyes. Surely he could not have gone so far so soon. The city at night, the fountain, the lights. We found him, in a milk bar of course. They had given him a chocolate malted, and he said he was not lost — he knew where he was.

Do you know now, Michael? Do you still know where you are?

But we are just ordinary people. I cry sometimes, but not too much. I am afraid that if I cry too much I may never be able to stop. All the sins, all the sorrows of all our lifetimes, are dammed in me. So I dig the soil, and I plant flowers — geraniums for summer colour, looking ahead, you see, beyond the storms of spring. Garden beds, filled and overflowing, spilling lobelia and alyssum, the honey flower, falling across the paths, like children's colouring books, the pinks and the purples sprawling out of the lines ...

— You see, Mrs Lynch, we feel that Michael is trying to tell us something in his drawings, particularly through his use of colour.

They thought there was something unhappy about Michael. Didn't I know?

— Yes, he doesn't like school.

— But.

— He would rather stay home and play in the garden with me.

There it was again, the sigh, shrug, half smile. You know that is not the way things are. Society does not allow ...

Her eyes tried to hold mine, confidentially. We have a duty to show him how things are. With plasticine and jelly moulds. The lines of her face squabbled for a sympathetic pose, but she looked tired, and her lips shaped trite phrases like 'peer-group pressure', and 'expectations', and 'social deviants'.

— Can you see there are some children not made for all the words you'll ever find?

In the spring, I plant the borders so they overflow with colour, geum and ageratum, nemesia and bees. Foxgloves poking ragged fingers to the sky ...

— Look! Daddy took a photo of me with raspberries on all my fingers. Like fairy bonnets!

Michael held his fingers out to me. Ten fingers, ten raspberries.

— Daddy took a photo!

He ate the raspberry bonnets from his fingers, one by one. What happened?

I could find the photograph still, but I shall not. It sits in the album on the shelf, waiting through the years to spill out the chaos of that raspberry summer. We milked the raspberries from their canes, and the juice ran clean and red over our tongues.

Each day you do what you have to do for that day. But the days cast a deep shadow back into the past, and we go picking around in the shade, looking for clues.

Christmas comes with the peppermint gums stripping their bark on to the front driveway, and even the crows are silent, like black mould on the bleached branches. That Christmas we saw what maybe the whole village already knew. How could they know and not tell us?

They brought him home in the police car, two of them, blue and huge, and Michael's drunken legs supported by burly arms.

Bad company.

Under-age drinking.

Peer-group pressure.

All the stereotypes. They cannot be true. This is Michael, he belongs to me. All those nights he ran away. But we always found him and brought him back. And he hated and fought and swore. But he was ours. Inside these four walls he was ours. The world could not get to him.

Neither could I.

This was my son. He could say these things to me. I should have split open with the meat-cleaver words he used on me. But the dam wall held.

So tall, so beautiful, his father's eyes. The words of hate from those childish lips.

And all the golden years fell away and cringed between us like a whipped cur.

In the summer, the flowers I planted in the spring storms begin to bloom, the godetia and the marigolds like a hundred little suns, and lemonbalm to attract the bees. The beds and borders hum in the heat and the colours drip and curdle under my eyelids, stinging. See what you plant in anticipation … shadows shading their tired eyes to see the future. All the time you only do what you think you ought to do. I remember planting and planting in the warm spring winds, hoping and planning and planting the future. Garden of Eden. Garden of Gethsemane.

I did not want to see Michael in the hospital, but they said he was still ours. A little boy again. Except for the head on the pillow, shadow-cheeked, I could not tell his body was in the bed. The shivering and sweating had stopped. His lips burned.

When I think of drug barons at all, I imagine them sitting beside their blue pools sipping expensive drinks under a sun umbrella, while their gardens explode in bloom around them, rhododendrons and azalea, whorls of fuchsia and green-shaven lawns. The garden feeds well on the bodies of sons like Michael, betrayed by the myth and lost in the compromise.

In the autumn they brought him home. And his eyes did not belong anymore. The world had left him, and our four walls were strait-jackets on a lost spirit.

The garden fades and shrivels against the cold east wind.

I found a syringe in his drawer and the truth pooling in his eyes.

The garden dies under its mat of mulch, and the cherry tree drips its leaves on the wet lawn. Raindrops cling like scared children to the arthritic fingers of the silver birch. The sun's rays have no strength to dry the grass, and the droplets sparkle in the cool wind.

Where is the strength that mothers always have?

I find it in Michael's brothers. Michael must not be allowed to compromise these last fruits, the final harvest.

I drove him back to the city. Lights drowned in the rain puddles smearing the pavement. I released him to the darkness where he belongs. Once he belonged to me.

In the winter when I lie in bed and listen in the dark, I know when the wind is blowing from the east. It swirls like the Pied Piper through the high branches of the peppermint gums, and bits of bark and twigs and gumnuts patter and snap on the iron roof, like little bones breaking. The east wind is so cold, blowing in across vast lonely reaches of sea-fog.

The sun leaves us early now, and the garden is barren. All that spring and summer work, hoeing, digging, mulching, planting, it all comes to winter. The ground is hard and cold, arid dead leaves clog the gutters. Sometimes I think of summer.

Now the paddocks bleed a pale light as the sun slips away. Orchards fold dark blankets across the hills. A shy drizzle creeps up the river, and I hear the black swans calling behind the mist, crying like lost children.

Are You   *Sarah Katherine Pidgeon*

Discussion

1   In one word, what do you think this story is about?

2   When Caroline realised that her parents were about to divorce, she felt suddenly that 'it didn't really matter' and that 'she could cope'. From what you have learnt about Caroline in the story, do you agree with her? Give reasons for your point of view.

3   Notice that the author makes good *use of detail* in this story. Read the story again and see what Sarah Katherine Pidgeon spends most of her time talking about. What is the effect of this approach? Would it not be more effective if she had poured forth Caroline's feelings onto the page?

Activities

1   It is the morning after. Caroline is back at school. What is the first line that she speaks to:
  - her mate, Jenny?
  - a boyfriend?
  - the school counsellor?

2   In a page of stage dialogue, write the scene in which Caroline's mother and father decide to break the news to her about the divorce. Remember that stage dialogue always works well if it contains a measure of conflict.

3 The story ends with Caroline saying to her parents: 'You're getting a divorce. — Aren't you?' Imagine that she is wrong. What is her father's reply to the question? Write a second half to this story, trying, as much as possible, to retain the style of the original.

The Toy Girl *Paula Clark*

Discussion

1 What happened in this story? Why did it happen? How do you know?

2 What kind of relationship existed between Paula and her guests?

3 We possess *five senses*, the senses of smell, sight, sound, taste and touch. When describing a scene, writers should not forget that there are five senses, and they should not necessarily be content with using only the most common senses of sight and sound. How many senses are used in the short short story *The Toy Girl*? Show how the use of each adds to the effectiveness of the description.

Activities

1 What were the first words spoken after Paula's mother and father came through the front door, and who spoke them?

2 Imagine that Helen decides to write a thank-you letter to Paula. What does she say?

3 Examine the structure of this story. It is very short. There is virtually no dialogue. It is the description of a scene experienced by someone slowly returning to consciousness. Try writing one of these yourself. A person slowly regains consciousness. Where is he/she? What has happened? Reveal the details slowly.

East Wind *Gillian Dawson*

Discussion

1 What happened to Michael? Tell the story from the first time he left home (when he was three) to the last time he left home.

2 What sort of a boy was Michael? What sort of a relationship did Michael have with his mother? What did Mrs Lynch do to Michael at the end of the story, and why?

3   What is the *tone* of this short short story? Re-read all the descriptions of gardens, plants, seasons and references to the elements in this story. Why are they given so much space in the story? How do these descriptive passages affect the tone of the story? (The 'tone' refers to the mood or manner in which a story is presented, and springs from the author's own attitude to the material.)

Activities

1   One day, long after Michael has gone, Mrs Lynch finds an old letter written by Michael, in the back of a cupboard. It is addressed to someone she had never heard of. In it, Michael talks about his family. What does he say? Write a page.

2   In pairs, briefly prepare, and then act out, an improvised scene in which a schoolmate challenges one of Michael's brothers on the subject of his runaway elder brother.

3   Teenage years are a difficult time of life. Adolescents are forced to face problems of many different kinds. Write a story about any teenage problem that concerns you. If you would like some starting points, here are three.
- A teenager changes schools half way through the year ...
- A teenager throws a party. The parents have gone out for the evening ...
- A teenager finds himself or herself pressured by others in the peer group to do something very much against his/her better judgement ...

Love Letter
Straight From
the Heart

Terry Tapp

Terry Tapp, an English writer, sold his first story to the *Evening News*, a London paper that printed a short story every day. In those days, Edward Campbell, the literary editor, gave great help to his writers. 'Remember that a short story is not just a story that is short', he wrote on one rejection slip. Other helpful comments were, 'Forget the purple writing', and 'You can't cheat the reader by saying it was only a dream'.

There were six letters on the doormat — four bills, one circular and one green envelope. It was, of course, the green envelope which caught Robert's eye.

He picked the bundle up and ambled through to the kitchen, systematically slitting the letters open with his thumb. Then he put the kettle on for a cup of tea, lit a cigarette and sat at the table.

Purposely teasing himself, he opened the accounts, read them and placed them to one side — envelopes in a neat pile ready for the waste bin. The circular came next and Robert spent a tantalising two minutes deciding that he did not require a set of 'see-as-you-cook' cards. Now for the green envelope.

At that moment the kettle whistled and, with a rueful grin, Robert went to the stove and poured the boiling water over the tea in the pot. His heart was pounding.

With not so much as a glance at the green envelope, he poured the milk into the cup, added sugar and waited for the tea to infuse. And all the while his stomach was knotted with a curious mixture of guilt and excitement.

'I'll write to you,' she had said.

'Do you think that wise?' he had asked anxiously.

'What is wise about love?' she had laughed.

Robert poured his tea and took the cup back to the table. After a sip or two, he could stand the tension no longer and he pulled the letter out.

My Darling, it started. *I promised you that I would write … but what can I say? I could say I love you, but the phrase is all used up nowadays: I adore you … I worship you. No, it means much more than that. To be terribly romantic, I think I would lay my life down for you if you asked it. I want, any way I can, to make you happy.*

Robert lit another cigarette, inhaling deeply.

Our stolen time together was an island in my life. I must see you again. God knows, it isn't often during a lifetime that two people meet and fall in love. For us to have met, like strangers lost in a big city, was a miracle and I cannot let it go at that.
I know you are married and I know you feel guilty about our affair, but I am helpless to stop myself pursuing you.

Ever yours,
Your unsigned lover.

Robert read it again and again. He drank his tea and smoked another cigarette and then read the letter through again, savouring each word like a fine, rare wine. Who would have guessed that he, a middle-aged executive would fall madly, crazily in love with a girl half his age?

It wasn't as if he was unhappily married either. Cynthia had been — still was — a good and loyal wife. He bit his lip, struggling against the guilt which surged through him.

Another cup of tea and another cigarette.

What would he do if she became too serious? Would he be prepared to give up everything for her?

Divorce? Oh, God, he thought. Not that.

Yes, he loved her, this gay slip of a girl, and she was obviously madly in love with him; but to give up everything, the home, the safe, stable marriage …

Yet again he read the letter, his thoughts clashing against his skull like steel pins until he could no longer think properly.

Did he love her? Did he love her more than he loved Cynthia? How can a man answer such a thing? They were separate loves, pigeon-holed, waterproof emotions which could not possibly be mixed. He would, no matter what, always love his wife. Yet, he could not deny it, he was like a schoolboy at the thought of spending more time with his new love.

As he placed another cigarette between his lips, Cynthia came into the kitchen to start the breakfast.

'Tea in the pot,' he said, as he always did.

She nodded, removed a cigarette from his pack and lit it.

'Just a boiled egg,' he told her in reply to her upraised eyebrows. Funny that Cynthia never had to speak. A look here, a nod there and that was all that was needed. He observed her anew.

Dressing gown, tatty slippers, hair not yet brushed. She stood over the stove, cigarette dangling from her lips, thoughts a million miles away. Yet, as soon as she had prepared his breakfast, it would take but ten or fifteen minutes to transform her. She would be washed, dressed in something smart and her make-up would be flawless. Robert grinned. It was a dilemma.

'What are you smiling at?' she asked suddenly.

'Nothing,' he said.

She shrugged. 'Did I hear the postman?'

'Yes,' he answered, suddenly realising that he was holding the green letter in his hands.

'Anything interesting?' she asked.

His heart went thump-thump-thump. 'Nothing much. Just a few bills and a circular.'

'Nothing else?'

'No.'

She placed the egg in the boiling water, noticed that the shell had cracked and said, 'Damn,' causing a cylinder of ash to fall from her cigarette into the boiling water.

Again she shrugged, then went over to the table and laid plates and knives and spoons. 'What's this?' she asked, picking up the green envelope. 'I thought you said it was only bills and things.'

'Nothing,' he replied, noting with some annoyance that his voice was trembling.

'It's a letter,' she said.

Robert pushed the corner of the green page deep into his pocket. 'Just business,' he told her. 'Anyway, you know we have this thing about reading each other's mail. This happens to be private.'

She held the envelope between forefinger and thumb as if it were infected. 'In that case,' she replied, 'perhaps you would be so kind as to tell me why you opened a letter which is addressed to me.'

Once in Love With Carla

Stan Moye

This is the story of four people, all from this village.

First Carla, the most beautiful girl in the world.

Then Fidel, rich old goat and hard businessman. Next Rosa, fat and plain, daughter of the innkeeper.

And lastly me, Jose, a handsome, young man of athletic … oh pardon, perhaps I overstate my case.

The sad business begins with Carla the beautiful making a decision that was to alter all of our lives.

She wanted to be rich (born at the other end of the village as well. How did a perfect blossom grow from such weeds?).

So she set out to follow a well-worn path. Have you heard the wise saying: 'If you don't inherit it, or earn it, or win it, then marry it.' You haven't? It's not surprising, I just invented it.

And who was the only one with money? Yes, Fidel the crabface. What a waste. There was I, all that any woman could desire, waiting, eating my heart out, but she ignored me.

What did I have? I had Rosa the ugly, always at my elbow — 'Jose, take some wine, Jose, come for a walk, Jose, do you like my dress?' And all while the light of my life was throwing herself at a walking bank.

Forgive me. The thought of her beauty and his money brings tears to my eyes. I love both.

Next comes the most heart-breaking part. I must bring myself to say it, though. Came the day they married, there was bright sunshine. If there was any justice it would have snowed, with earth tremors.

Such rejoicing. Some danced. Well, to be truthful, all the village danced, but not me. There was singing all night but I did not sing. All I could do was be brave, hide my wounds, and drink wine. Of course, it was Fidel's wine and that nearly prevented me from taking it.

But I am a man of strong character and I forced myself. And so Carla, the woman I loved, went to live with the old skinflint in the big house on the hill.

I waited to see her become unhappy with her bargain but, as I sit here, I swear she looked, first of all, content. Yes, that is the word, content — and as time passed, even happy.

Sometimes, at the end of the day, she would meet him as he closed his office and they would walk slowly back up the hill in the cool of the evening.

How I watched them. The sight of her olive skin and white teeth as she threw back her head to laugh at something he said was agony to me. And he — he actually looked twenty years younger. No, I lie — ten years.

If she does that for an ancient mummy like him, what could she have done for me? I thought. And then came a thought to console me. To be married to Carla and be poor would be bliss. But to be married to the widow Carla and be rich would be paradise.

How long could he last? Surely she must kill him with love. A young, beautiful wife must be kept — happy, if you know what I mean. Think of his heart! While this was going on in my mind, Rosa was always there, 'Do you like my hair? Take me up the mountain (and I admit there had been some walks up the mountain). Papa wants to meet you!'

Meet me! All my life I have known him and now he wants to meet me! The woman was madly in love with me — desperate. But it is quite understandable. Women are very weak. Then, my friend, one glorious day Fidel dropped dead. 'Hooray — God rest his soul,' I shout.

Now soon will be my chance. But I am a man of propriety. I wait. One week, two weeks, three whole weeks. Then I make my move. She was more beautiful than ever in black. 'Good morning, Carla,' I say, 'may I extend my …'

'Good day,' she says, not even looking at me. 'Drive on,' and away goes the coach leaving me in a cloud of dust.

Me! — the one who has saved himself for her (well practically), fought off the advances of others (most of the time), left with shame in the middle of the village.

I suddenly see I have made a terrible mistake. This woman is not in love with his money, she actually loved Fidel. How can this happen? What can I do? How can I ever reach her? The woman is deaf and blind with grief.

Feeling I needed support I staggered into the inn. It was a black day, for here waited Rosa's father eager to discuss his daughter with someone.

We talked like civilized men. So intense did we become that, at the climax of our discussion, he buried a meat axe into the table in order to make his point. That man had an arm like a bull's leg. And then this big generous man, who did not know when to stop giving, gave me his most treasured possession, his daughter Rosa.

Now I am a very reasonable man and can understand the views of someone that size, so I accept.

That day I survived two momentous events. My beloved spurned me and I was given a wife.

The years have passed and we are all older. Carla still lives in the big house, the one with the iron gates. You see? From her radiates the same contentment and inner happiness.

She married for gain but found most unexpectedly, love.

I am now the landord of the inn and live with Rosa and our ten children. Yes, it's true, ten. Rosa is still a very large, plain woman but she has many hidden attributes.

I, too, married and then found love later. Perhaps we are guided along life's path after all.

What? Is that all there is to my story I hear you ask?

What did you expect, family feuds, gunfire, horse whippings? This is a quiet village where a man has time to drink a little wine and watch his children grow. Nothing happens here — nowadays.

The
Grasshopper
and the
Bell Cricket

Yasunari Kawabata
Translated by Lane Dunlop from the Japanese

Yasunari Kawabata was born in 1899 in Japan. His stories are full of the Japanese love for the delicate and beautiful, and he wrote about love, loneliness, the passing of time, and the tensions between the traditional values and the modern influences in Japanese society. He was awarded the Nobel Prize for Literature in 1968. Four years later he committed suicide.

Walking along the tile-roofed wall of the university, I turned aside and approached the upper school. Behind the whiteboard fence of the school playground, from a dusky clump of bushes under the black cherry trees, an insect's voice could be heard. Walking more slowly and listening to that voice, and furthermore reluctant to part with it, I turned right so as not to leave the playground behind. When I turned to the left, the fence gave way to an embankment planted with orange trees. At the corner, I exclaimed with surprise. My eyes gleaming at what they saw up ahead, I hurried forward with short steps.

At the base of the embankment was a bobbing cluster of beautiful varicolored lanterns, such as one might see at a festival in a remote country village. Without going any farther, I knew that it was a group of children on an insect chase among the bushes of the embankment. There were about twenty lanterns. Not only were there crimson, pink, indigo, green, purple, and yellow lanterns, but one lantern glowed with five colors at once. There were even some little red store-bought lanterns. But most of the lanterns were beautiful square ones which the children had made themselves with love and care. The bobbing lanterns, the coming together of children on this lonely slope — surely it was a scene from a fairy tale?

One of the neighborhood children had heard an insect sing on this slope one night. Buying a red lantern, he had come back the next night to find the insect. The night after that, there was another child. This new child could not buy a lantern. Cutting out the back and front of a small carton and papering it, he placed a candle on the bottom and fastened a string to the top. The number of children grew to five, and then to seven. They learned how to color the paper that they stretched over the windows of the cutout cartons, and to draw pictures on it. Then these wise child-artists, cutting out round, three-cornered, and lozenge leaf shapes in the cartons, coloring each little window a different color, with circles and diamonds, red and green, made a single and whole decorative pattern. The child with the red lantern discarded it as a tasteless object that could be bought at a store. The child who had made his own lantern threw it away because the design was too simple. The pattern of light that one had had in hand the night before was unsatisfying the morning after. Each day, with cardboard, paper, brush, scissors, pen-knife, and glue, the children made new lanterns out of their hearts and minds. Look at my lantern! Be the most unusually beautiful! And each night, they had gone out on their insect hunts. These were the twenty children and their beautiful lanterns that I now saw before me.

Wide-eyed, I loitered near them. Not only did the square lanterns have old-fashioned patterns and flower shapes, but the names of the children who had made them were cut out in squared letters of the syllabary. Different from the painted-over red lanterns, others (made of thick cutout cardboard) had their designs drawn onto the paper windows, so that the candle's light seemed to emanate from the form and color of the design itself. The lanterns brought out the shadows of the bushes like dark light. The children crouched eagerly on the slope wherever they heard an insect's voice.

'Does anyone want a grasshopper?' A boy, who had been peering into a bush about thirty feet away from the other children, suddenly straightened up and shouted.

'Yes! Give it to me!' Six or seven children came running up. Crowding behind the boy who had found the grasshopper, they peered into the bush. Brushing away their outstretched hands and spreading out his arms, the boy stood as if guarding the bush where the insect was. Waving the lantern in his right hand, he called again to the other children.

'Does anyone want a grasshopper? A grasshopper!'

'I do! I do!' Four or five more children came running up. It seemed you could not catch a more precious insect than a grasshopper. The boy called out a third time.

'Doesn't anyone want a grasshopper?'

Two or three more children came over.

'Yes. I want it.'

It was a girl, who just now had come up behind the boy who'd dis-covered the insect. Lightly turning his body, the boy gracefully bent for-ward. Shifting the lantern to his left hand, he reached his right hand into the bush.

'It's a grasshopper.'

'Yes. I'd like to have it.'

The boy quickly stood up. As if to say 'Here!' he thrust out his fist that held the insect at the girl. She, slipping her left wrist under the string of her lantern, enclosed the boy's fist with both hands. The boy quietly opened his fist. The insect was transferred to between the girl's thumb and index finger.

'Oh! It's not a grasshopper. It's a bell cricket.' The girl's eyes shone as she looked at the small brown insect.

'It's a bell cricket! It's a bell cricket!' The children echoed in an envi-ous chorus.

'It's a bell cricket. It's a bell cricket.'

Glancing with her bright intelligent eyes at the boy who had given her the cricket, the girl opened the little insect cage hanging at her side and released the cricket in it.

'It's a bell cricket.'

'Oh, it's a bell cricket,' the boy who'd captured it muttered. Holding up the insect cage close to his eyes, he looked inside it. By the light of his beautiful many-colored lantern, also held up at eye level, he glanced at the girl's face.

Oh, I thought. I felt slightly jealous of the boy, and sheepish. How silly of me not to have understood his actions until now! Then I caught my breath in surprise. Look! It was something on the girl's breast which neither the boy who had given her the cricket, nor she who had accepted it, nor the children who were looking at them noticed.

In the faint greenish light that fell on the girl's breast, wasn't the name 'Fujio' clearly discernible? The boy's lantern, which he held up alongside the girl's insect cage, inscribed his name, cut out in the green papered aperture, onto her white cotton kimono. The girl's lantern, which dangled loosely from her wrist, did not project its pattern so clearly, but still one could make out, in a trembling patch of red on the boy's waist, the name 'Kiyoko'. This chance interplay of red and green — if it was chance or play — neither Fujio nor Kiyoko knew about.

Even if they remembered forever that Fujio had given her the cricket and that Kiyoko had accepted it, not even in dreams would Fujio ever know that his name had been written in green on Kiyoko's breast or that Kiyoko's name had been inscribed in red on his waist, nor would Kiyoko ever know that Fujio's name had been inscribed in green on her breast or that her own name had been written in red on Fujio's waist.

Fujio! Even when you have become a young man, laugh with pleasure at a girl's delight when, told that it's a grasshopper, she is given a bell cricket; laugh with affection at a girl's chagrin when, told that it's a bell cricket, she is given a grasshopper.

Even if you have the wit to look by yourself in a bush away from the other children, there are not many bell crickets in the world. Probably you will find a girl like a grasshopper whom you think is a bell cricket.

And finally, to your clouded, wounded heart, even a true bell cricket will seem like a grasshopper. Should that day come, when it seems to you that the world is only full of grasshoppers, I will think it a pity that you have no way to remember tonight's play of light, when your name was written in green by your beautiful lantern on a girl's breast.

Love Letters Straight From the Heart   *Terry Tapp*

Discussion

1   What was Cynthia thinking about, do you suppose, with her 'thoughts a million miles away'? Invent the details.

2   What kind of a marriage did Robert and Cynthia have? How do you know? Talk about specific details when answering these questions.

3   A *simile* is a figure of speech in which something from one field of experience is said to be similar to something in another field. Similes are recognised by the flagwords 'like' or 'as' (or 'as ... as'). Find four similes in 'Love Letters Straight From the Heart', and explain what each one adds to the effectiveness of the story.

Activities

1   'In that case,' she replied, 'perhaps you would be so kind as to tell me why you opened a letter which is addressed to me.' What happens next? Devise three possible directions in which this story might go.

2   Write half a page in which Cynthia explains to Robert exactly what is going on, and why.

3   Very often even those people we think we know best may well appear as strangers to us. Write a story of a marriage where one partner suddenly realises, after 30 years, that the other partner is one of the following:
- a spy for a foreign power
- a criminal
- married to someone else.

Once in Love With Carla   *Stan Moye*

Discussion

1   Why did Rosa's father bury his meat axe into the table during the course of his 'civilised' discussion with Jose?

2   What sort of a person was Jose? How do you know? Refer to the details and quote from the story in your answer.

3   A *theme* is an underlying idea which runs through a piece of writing. What would you say was the theme of this short short story? State it clearly in one sentence.

Activities

1   Jose is a confident young man, but Carla does not fall for his charm and line of talk. Write a passage of dialogue in which a bystander falls for the 'line' of a confidence trickster.

2   Perform a dramatic reading of this story. One person must read the story. The others mime the roles of Carla, Fidel, Rosa, Jose and Rosa's father as they come into the story. Make it entertaining.

3   Part of the enjoyment of this story comes about because our young and attractive storyteller does not know what he wants although he thinks he does, and thinks he knows whom he wants although he does not. In real life, love is not the glamorous thing it is made out to be in glossy magazines or in the movies. It is far more unpredictable. Write a story of an unexpected or unlikely love affair. Make it realistic; make it honest.

The Grasshopper and the Bell Cricket   *Yasunari Kawabata*

Discussion

1   What is the significance of the grasshopper and the bell cricket in this story? Why is the moment of the giving of the insect such an important and precious one?

2   In the last three paragraphs of the story, we look ahead to the lives of Fujio and Kiyoko. What ideas are contained in these final lines of the story?

3   Kawabata makes great use of *repetition* in this short short story. What is the effect of the repeating of certain sentences and phrases throughout this tale? Examine them individually.

Activities

1   'The Grasshopper and the Bell Cricket' has been referred to by Charles Baxter, an American writer, as 'one of the best stories written by anyone anywhere.' How do you react to this statement? Write a paragraph.

2   Yasunari Kawabata writes in a very distinctive style in this story. Write about an incident from your own life, in the third person, adopting the style of 'The Grasshopper and the Bell Cricket'.

3   Write a story inspired by one of the following lines.
   • 'Even if you have the wit to look by yourself in a bush away from the other children, there are not many bell crickets in the world.'
   • 'Probably you will find a girl like a grasshopper whom you think is a bell cricket.'
   • 'And finally, to your clouded, wounded heart, even a true bell cricket will seem like a grasshopper.'

Day to
Remember

James Clavell

James Clavell was born in Australia but brought up in England. The war influenced him greatly. In 1942 he was captured by the Japanese and sent to Changi prison, and this experience gave him material for his first novel *King Rat*. His other novels include *Tai-Pan* and *Shogun*. Later he went into films and wrote the screenplays for *The Great Escape, To Sir With Love* and *The Last Valley*.

The Colonel's wife was lying in the rubble of an old London house laid waste by a V-2.

The November wind squalled and cut as only an English wind can cut, and she felt the freezing rain on her face.

But she was glad of the cold. It deadened the hurt that now surrounded her.

Around there were screams and pain and the sound of flames nearby — and far off, the sound of approaching sirens.

I hope I don't burn, she thought, I don't mind dying, but I don't want to burn first. What's today? Oh, my, it's Sunday. Of course, I'd just got back from church. You're getting quite silly Maudie. Well, Sunday's a good day to die on. The little thought comforted her.

She tried to move. She could not feel her legs at all. Nor her right arm. But the left moved free, and she watched as it lifted itself above her, and the rain ran down her fingers across the little gold band and dropped on to her face.

The fingers touched her face then brushed a little of the rubble away and moved a strand of grey hair from her eyes.

She began to wonder about the other tenants. Did they get out of their bedsitters before the V-2 hit? And what about dear little Felix, the kitten, the joy of her solitude. Maudie remembered that she had had him in her arms near the stove pouring some milk, just before. 'Kitty! kitty!'

'No need to worry,' she said aloud for she had been alone so long she often talked to herself, 'kittens have nine lives.'

'They're luckier than humans. Or perhaps unluckier. Perhaps it is better to have only one life.'

There was something that she had to remember. Something important. What could that be? Oh, yes. She'd left the gas fire on! Now that's a silly thing to do. Dangerous. And, oh yes! The rations! Her week's rations had been on the table. What a waste.

Such a lovely lamb chop that she'd saved her whole week's coupon for.

Maudie, that'll teach you a lesson. Eat your rations while you've got them.

That thought pleased her. And another; no more queues or ration books or being cold. She hated the cold and loved India. Ah, those were good days, in the Indian Army. The warmth and enough food and the servants and such lovely dances …

The rain fell harder now and she had to close her eyes. Somewhere there was an all-clear siren. The sound of fire was nearer … nearer than before.

Pain came and took her and used her, and then the terror of dying engulfed her and she shouted, 'HELPPPPPP!' But she made no sound at all.

Get hold of yourself, Maudie. There's no need to be afraid. There's a God in Heaven and, all in all, you've been as good as a human can be. So there is nothing to fear. Perhaps you won't die after all. You must be patient and wait and see.

So she gathered herself and settled to wait and as she waited she prayed.

Most of her prayer was for William, her eldest son, now part of the armoured horde that was sweeping the enemy away.

Blasted Germans. Twice we've had to fight them. Well let's hope we do a good job this time. I lost my father and my uncle in the Great War — and now in the Second — my youngest, my George, a Spitfire death, and my husband, my Richard, lost somewhere in the East, 'missing, presumed dead'. So many deaths. Dear God in Heaven, what for?

'Here, kitty, kitty.'

When the war began, Maudie had been glad for Richard. Peace-time promotion was so slow, and in war, well, he was trained for war. With luck, a General's crossed swords, like his father before him.

But he was captured at Singapore and promotions were being swallowed up by juniors.

Still — if he was alive, if he lived out the war — even now he could get his General's swords.

Those meant security, and the house that they had always wanted to buy — the house they had seen so many years ago, the house that was far above their means — the house that she bought two years ago.

'I just had to, Richard. The owner was leaving England, and it was so reasonable …'

An ancient Elizabethan house. Rolling gardens and lawns and oaks and a wisteria and a little bridge and diamond windows peeping out so prettily. Chadlott's Close. Their home.

She had taken out all their savings and the deed had been drawn up and she had promised to pay five thousand more pounds over years and years but that did not matter for there was all the time in the world.

And one day Chadlott's would belong to William and his children and his children's children.

Then a year ago she had come back to London to sign more papers and give more money, but that was good for she could just manage if she was careful.

And then she had gone home and got off the train and walked the four miles and all the yew trees were smashed down and the roots of the wisteria were torn from the earth and the house was no more and blown apart and the beams were gutted with fire and the swathes of lawn were holes, holes, holes, and over Chadlott's there was smoke.

Chadlott's was dead. Dead.

That night she had died too, sitting on a murdered tree, her tears watering the earth. She got up and never returned.

And, now thinking of the unnecessary obliteration of such beauty, she screamed her hate at the devil's spawn who started the war and destroyed Chadlott's.

And she cursed them with her whole being for taking the life of Chadlott's and letting her live.

Curse you, curse you, curse you!

Not for my father or my uncle or my son, or my son-in-law or his son, or my husband, or for me — humans are expendable and it is right that men should defend these shores and women should suffer.

But ten thousand million curses for Chadlott's Close.

For nothing ever, ever, can rebuild or re-life that which had seen four hundred years of life. Nothing. Not even God.

'Kitty, kitty, here kitty.'

I don't mind dying, but I hate dying without seeing you all again. I wish I could see you again, all of my children and most my Richard — who is most my child, my old, old child.

Poor Chadlott's my dear one.

'Here kitty … here …'

She died in the rubble there under the rain and the wind, deep in the rubble. The kitten still nestled into the cradle of her shattered right arm. Cold long since.

The Clearing

Martyn Hereward

Martyn Hereward was born in England, and travelled widely in his youth. In 1969 he settled in Australia, where he married and now has three children. The idea for 'The Clearing' came after a visit to New Guinea, where he heard many stories about the war from farmers and settlers.

I stepped into the clearing and the cicadas suddenly stopped singing. I wondered how they knew to do that. The silence seemed to swell inside my head. The next thing I knew I was spinning like a top, going round and round in slow motion. Then I was lying flat on my face, my mouth full of moss and bark. I wanted to laugh then but I could not move.

When Curly copped one from the Jap I could see he was hurt bad. He just lay there. I thought to myself, the poor bastard can't get up, I'm gonna have to go in there and get him. I could see where the shot had come from, clump of trees on the edge of the forest, thick and green it was. Bastards, I thought. Just sitting up there waiting. I didn't hang around, just dropped to the ground and started slithering, snake-like through the undergrowth. When I got to the edge of the clearing I popped my head up to have a bit of a look. As far as I could see Curly hadn't moved, he was lying with his face in the dirt. There was about twenty metres between me and him so I took it careful, going slow like and keeping my head down. There was a bit of bushy scrub and some long grass but that was about all, so off I set remembering everything from training and thinking bloody oath I never thought I'd be doing this in the middle of the bloody jungle in bloody New Guinea. I don't think there was more shots fired then, but I wouldn't swear to it for I was hold-ing my breath and praying that the Japs hadn't seen me, course I knew they had. Suddenly I was through the grass and there was Curly, he was spluttering a bit and there was blood in his mouth but he was breathing all right. I tried to get his pack off him but it wouldn't come free because of the way he was lying so I cut the straps and shoved it away. Then I rolled him over, slow and careful. Poor bastard had got one high up in the chest, there was blood everywhere but there was nothing I could do, so I thought bloody hell I'm going to have to drag him back to cover. I didn't know if I could. He looked at me and I think he knew who I was but he couldn't talk so I said, take it easy mate we'll have you out of here and he sort of smiled. I tried to push him but he wouldn't shift, so I knew then I was going to have to stand up if I wanted to get him moving. Well, I thought, it might as well be now as later, the poor bastard's losing blood so I said a quick prayer to God knows who, took a hold of his uniform, jumped up and dug in my heels.

There's always one, isn't there? One bright swivel-eyed bastard who insists on playing the hero and covering himself in glory. Everyone knows the orders. They're standing orders. Captain Maitland and I had made that patently clear. 'No bloody heroics,' I told them. 'We know the Japs are up there somewhere. We move slowly. We play it by the book.'

Not an easy job, damn it, especially as some of these bright boys from the country think they're straight out of the comic books. Give them a uniform and a gun and they think they're straight out of the comic books.

I've had trouble with O'Brien before. He was the one who gave me some lip the first day we arrived in this God-forsaken country. 'Ease up, Sergeant,' he said. 'This is New bloody Guinea not New South Wales.'

I thought, right you bastard, you'll keep. I've met his sort before. Bloody barrack room clowns who join up and think they know it all. If I had my way I'd break both his bloody legs. That'd send him home in a hurry. I looked across at Captain Maitland, but he didn't seem to be listening. He's a good bloke, the captain, don't get me wrong, but he's no soldier. He doesn't concentrate for one thing. I mean who else would walk into that clearing like he did? Back at camp they say he's got too much imagination. If you ask me, I don't think he's got enough.

'Get back!' I shouted at O'Brien, but he didn't take a blind bit of notice.

I got my gun out and thought to myself, the bastard has got to stick his head up soon if he's going to do any good, and then the Japs are going to blow him out of the clearing. I shouted to the rest of the men to give him cover and to take aim at the clump of trees on the far side of the clearing. We knew they were in there somewhere.

For a long while nothing happened.

Then the grass parted and Private O'Brien stood up. He was leaning backwards and trying to drag something through the bush.

'Covering fire!' I shouted, and all hell broke loose. I let off a couple of rounds myself, and I could see the smoke over by the forest. It didn't last long, I guess the Japs realised we were on to them and moved away fast. When I looked back at the clearing there was nothing to be seen.

I was quite close to the clearing when the captain was hit. It was beautiful. He raised one arm high in the air and twisted like a fast bowler appealing to the umpire or a puppet spinning slowly round as the strings went slack. There was a hollow crack as the air went out of him, then he buckled at the knees and down he went. There was no other sound. A red rose began to appear on his right shoulder like some rare medal as he fell.

It was very quiet. The jungle steamed, and the hot stench of decay weighed heavily on tree, fern and man. It was two o'clock in the afternoon.

I wiped the sweat out of my eyes.

I knew that Pat O'Brien would go in after him. Pat was like that: a doer, a scout, a tough kid from Ireland with all the hard edges still on him. His eyes were deep blue and reminded you of the oceans on a clear day and his hair was a bird's nest after it had been raided by small boys. When you saw Pat, you smiled.

Pat made his way towards the captain, wriggling in the undergrowth. I watched the grasses sway, then stop. The forest held its breath. There was no breeze. The birds folded their wings and waited.

When the firing began I saw it all. Pat stood up with his back to us. He was bent over as if he was hauling a sack of coal across the back yard. A blaze of red greeted us from under the tall gums across the clearing. Pat was still standing. I heard Sergeant Fallon barking out orders behind me and then more gunfire. Still Pat stood, the grasses waving at his feet like the swell of the tide on Bondi beach. He seemed to be caught up in the heat, a blur, a smudge of shadow, and then he buckled up. He was thrown backwards. His legs lurched forwards, but his body snapped backwards.

I saw it all.

I had not picked up my rifle through the whole incident. Pat's legs were broken, but they were broken from the back.

I tried to tell Private O'Brien about my arm but I couldn't make any sound. I was ashamed of myself. It was odd but I couldn't feel any pain. After a while I couldn't see Private O'Brien any more. I lay there and stared up at the cloudless blue sky and wondered if we were winning the war.

Then all around me, as one, the cicadas resumed their chorus.

Gregory

Panos Ioannides

*Translated by Marion Byron Raizis and Catherine Raizis
from the Greek*

Panos Ioannides was born in 1935 in Cyprus. As well as writing short stories,
he has written stage plays, radio scripts and television documentaries.
'Gregory' is based on a story told to him by a Cypriot guerilla about a young
English soldier held hostage and later executed during Cyprus' struggle for
independence in the 1950s.

My hand was sweating as I held the pistol. The curve of the trigger was
biting against my finger.

Facing me, Gregory trembled.

His whole being was beseeching me, 'Don't!'

Only his mouth did not make a sound. His lips were squeezed tight.
If it had been me, I would have screamed, shouted, cursed.

The soldiers were watching ...

The day before, during a brief meeting, they had each given their
opinions: 'It's tough luck, but it has to be done. We've got no choice.'

The order from Headquarters was clear: 'As soon as Lieutenant
Rafel's execution is announced, the hostage Gregory is to be shot and his
body must be hanged from a telegraph pole in the main street as an
exemplary punishment.'

It was not the first time that I had to execute a hostage in this war. I
had acquired experience, thanks to Headquarters which had kept
entrusting me with these delicate assignments. Gregory's case was precisely the sixth.

The first time, I remember, I vomited. The second time I got sick
and had a headache for days. The third time I drank a bottle of rum. The
fourth, just two glasses of beer. The fifth time I joked about it, 'This little
guy, with the big pop-eyes, won't be much of a ghost!'

But why, dammit, when the day came did I have to start thinking that I'm not so tough, after all? The thought had come at exactly the wrong time and spoiled all my disposition to do my duty.

You see, this Gregory was such a miserable little creature, such a puny thing, such a nobody, damn him.

That very morning, although he had heard over the loudspeakers that Rafel had been executed, he believed that we would spare his life because we had been eating together so long.

'Those who eat from the same mess tins and drink from the same water canteen,' he said, 'remain good friends no matter what.'

And a lot more of the same sort of nonsense.

He was a silly fool — we had smelled that out the very first day Headquarters gave him to us. The sentry guarding him had got dead drunk and had dozed off. The rest of us with exit permits had gone from the barracks. When we came back, there was Gregory sitting by the sleeping sentry and thumbing through a magazine.

'Why didn't you run away, Gregory?' we asked, laughing at him, several days later.

And he answered, 'Where would I go in this freezing weather? I'm O.K. here.'

So we started teasing him.

'You're dead right. The accommodations here are splendid ...'

'It's not bad here,' he replied. 'The barracks where I used to be are like a sieve. The wind blows in from every side ...'

We asked him about his girl. He smiled.

'Maria is a wonderful person,' he told us. 'Before I met her she was engaged to a no-good fellow, a pig. He gave her up for another girl. Then nobody in the village wanted to marry Maria. I didn't miss my chance. So what if she is second-hand. Nonsense. Peasant ideas, my friend. She's beautiful and good-hearted. What more could I want? And didn't she load me with watermelons and cucumbers every time I passed by her vegetable garden? Well, one day I stole some cucumbers and melons and watermelons and I took them to her. 'Maria,' I said, 'from now on I'm going to take care of you.' She started crying and then me, too. But ever since that day she has given me lots of trouble — jealousy. She wouldn't let me go even to my mother's. Until the day I was recruited, she wouldn't let me go far from her apron strings. But that was just what I wanted ...'

He used to tell this story over and over, always with the same words, the same commonplace gestures. At the end he would have a good laugh and start gulping from his water jug.

His tongue was always wagging! When he started talking, nothing could stop him. We used to listen and nod our heads, not saying a word.

But sometimes, as he was telling us about his mother and family problems, we couldn't help wondering, 'Eh, well, these people have the same headaches in their country as we've got.'

Strange, isn't it!

Except for his talking too much, Gregory wasn't a bad fellow. He was a marvellous cook. Once he made us some apple tarts, so delicious we licked the platter clean. And he could sew, too. He used to sew on all our buttons, patch our clothes, darn our socks, iron our ties, wash our clothes …

How the devil could you kill such a friend?

Even though his name was Gregory and some people on his side had killed one of ours, even though we had left wives and children to go to war against him and his kind — but how can I explain? He was our friend. He actually liked us! A few days before, hadn't he killed with his own bare hands a scorpion that was climbing up my leg? He could have let it send me to hell!

'Thanks, Gregory!' I said then, 'Thank God who made you …'

When the order came, it was like a thunderbolt. Gregory was to be shot, it said, and hanged from a telegraph pole as an exemplary punishment.

We got together inside the barracks. We sent Gregory to wash some underwear for us.

'It ain't right.'

'What is right?'

'Our duty!'

'Shit!'

'If you dare, don't do it! They'll drag you to court-martial and then bang-bang …'

Well, of course. The right thing is to save your skin. That's only logical. It's either your skin or his. His, of course, even if it was Gregory, the fellow you've been sharing the same plate with, eating with your fingers, and who was washing your clothes that very minute.

What could I do? That's war. We had seen worse things.

So we set the hour.

We didn't tell him anything when he came back from the washing. He slept peacefully. He snored for the last time. In the morning, he heard the news over the loudspeaker and he saw that we looked gloomy and he began to suspect that something was up. He tried talking to us, but he got no answers and then he stopped talking.

He just stood there and looked at us, stunned and lost …

Now, I'll squeeze the trigger. A tiny bullet will rip through his chest. Maybe I'll lose my sleep tonight but in the morning I'll wake up alive.

Gregory seems to guess my thoughts. He puts out his hand and asks, 'You're kidding, friend! Aren't you kidding?'

What a jackass! Doesn't he deserve to be cut to pieces? What a thing to ask at such a time. Your heart is about to burst and he's asking if you're kidding. How can a body be kidding about such a thing? Idiot! This is no time for jokes. And you, if you're such a fine friend, why don't you make things easier for us? Help us kill you with fewer qualms? You would get angry — curse our Virgin, our God — if you'd try to escape it would be much easier for us and for you.

So it is now.

Now, Mr Gregory, you are going to pay for your stupidities wholesale. Because you didn't escape the day the sentry fell asleep; because you didn't escape yesterday when we sent you all alone to the laundry — we did it on purpose, you idiot! Why didn't you let me die from the sting of the scorpion?

So now don't complain. It's all your fault, nitwit.

Eh? What's happening to him now?

Gregory is crying. Tears flood his eyes and trickle down over his clean-shaven cheeks. He is turning his face and pressing his forehead against the wall. His back is shaking as he sobs. His hands cling, rigid and helpless, to the wall.

Now is my best chance, now that he knows there is no other solution and turns his face from us.

I squeeze the trigger.

Gregory jerks. His back stops shaking up and down.

I think I've finished him! How easy it is ... But suddenly he starts crying out loud, his hands claw at the wall and try to pull it down. He screams, 'No, no ...'

I turn to the others. I expect them to nod, 'That's enough.'

They nod, 'What are you waiting for?'

I squeeze the trigger again.

The bullet smashed into his neck. A thick spray of blood spurts out.

Gregory turns. His eyes are all red. He lunges at me and starts punching me with his fists.

'I hate you, hate you ...' he screams.

I emptied the barrel. He fell and grabbed my leg as if he wanted to hold on.

He died with a terrible spasm. His mouth was full of blood and so were my boots and socks.

We stood quietly, looking at him.

When we came to, we stooped and picked him up. His hands were frozen and wouldn't let my legs go.

I still have their imprints, red and deep, as if made by a hot knife.
'We will hang him tonight,' the men said.
'Tonight or now?' they said.
I turned and looked at them one by one.
'Is that what you all want?' I asked.
They gave me no answer.
'Dig a grave,' I said.

Headquarters did not ask for a report the next day or the day after. The top brass were sure that we had obeyed them and had left him swinging from a pole.

They didn't care to know what happened to that Gregory, alive or dead.

Day to Remember   *James Clavell*

Discussion

1   What happened to the Colonel's wife after she returned home from church? Discuss her movements in detail.

2   What sort of a woman was the Colonel's wife? How do you know? Go into some detail in your discussion and refer closely to the story.

3   The use of *contrast* can be a very effective writing technique. What use does Clavell make of contrast here, and how does it contribute to the effectiveness of this short short story? Pick out specific examples of contrast in your answer.

Activities

1   Working from the description in the story, draw a rough sketch of the colonel's wife and her immediate surroundings after the landing of the V-2.

2   Imagine that William, Maudie's son, returns to his London home two days after the incident described here. In a page of writing, describe the scene that confronts him and his reaction to it. Concentrate (as Clavell does) on descriptive detail rather than turgid emotional prose. It is much more effective.

3 The war is over. William has settled down in a small London flat. One day a bent and bedraggled figure shuffles down the street and knocks on the door. It is his father. What happens next?

The Clearing   *Martyn Hereward*

Discussion

1 Who killed Private O'Brien, and why? How do you know?

2 Re-tell the events of 'The Clearing' clearly, briefly, in chronological order and in your own words.

3 **a** From how many *points of view* is this story told? Who, exactly, are the speakers, and what do we learn about each of them?
  b Who would you most/least like to have as your next-door neighbour, and why?

Activities

1 Analyse the language used by each of the characters in this story. How does each soldier use words? Discuss actual words and phrases used by each man, and show how these give insights into the individual characters involved in this incident.

2 Imagine that another soldier (of either side) also witnesses the events described in this short short story. How does he see the incident? Write a page, re-telling the story from his point of view. (If he is a Japanese soldier, ask an interpreter to translate his report into English!)

3 Write a war story set in the twentieth century in which not one shot is fired.

Gregory   *Panos Ioannides*

Discussion

1 Did the speaker obey the orders from Headquarters or not? What were his reasons for doing as he did?

2 What sort of a man was Gregory? How do you know? Go into some detail in your discussion and refer closely to the story.

3 A *metaphor* is a figure of speech in which an expression from one field of experience is used to say something in another field. A metaphor goes one step further than a simile and makes the comparison a direct one, omitting the words 'like' or 'as'. Pick out some examples of metaphor from 'Gregory', and show how the author has used them to heighten the drama of the story.

Activities

1   Write a brief review of a war film that has affected you.

2   Imagine that, after the shooting of Gregory, the executioner drafts a report of the incident for the official files at Headquarters. He also writes a letter to his wife about the affair. Write both the report and the letter. In what ways do they differ?

3   This story focuses on one relatively insignificant incident and uses it to make an observation about war and the people who are caught up in it. Try this for yourself. Choose an incident, preferably away from the front lines. Decide upon the point of view of the story, and centre it firmly around the single chosen incident. Here are three suggestions.
    • A nervous new recruit shoots himself in the foot.
    • A tough private is caught with the personal belongings, including the private diary, of an enemy soldier.
    • A corporal goes missing, and his disappearance is a mystery.

HUMOUR

Through the
Wilderness

Michael Frayn

Michael Frayn was born in England in 1933. He has turned his hand to writing of all kinds, and has been a novelist, dramatist, humourist and journalist. Witty and entertaining, he has written successful plays, for example, *Noises Off*, and experimental novels, which include *The Tin Man* and *A Very Private Life*.

It is nice now that all you boys have got cars of your own (*said Mother*). You know how much it means to me when the three of you drive down to see me like this, and we can all have a good old chatter together.

JOHN: That's right, Mother. So, as I was saying, Howard, I came down today through Wroxtead and Sudstow.

HOWARD: Really? I always come out through Dorris Hill and West Hatcham.

RALPH: I find I tend to turn off at the traffic lights in Manor Park Road myself and follow the 43 bus route through to the White Hart at Broylesden.

MOTHER: Ralph always was the adventurous one.

JOHN: Last time I tried forking right just past the police station in Broylesden High Street. I wasn't very impressed with it as a route, though.

HOWARD: Weren't you? That's interesting. I've occasionally tried cutting through the Broylesden Heath Estate. Then you can either go along Mottram Road South or Creese End Broadway. I think it's handy to have the choice.

RALPH: Of course, much the prettiest way for my money is to carry on into Hangmore and go down past the pickles factory in Sunnydeep Lane.

MOTHER: Your father and I once saw Lloyd George going down Sunnydeep Lane in a *wheelbarrow* ...

HOWARD: Did you, Mother? I'm not very keen on the Sunnydeep Lane way personally. I'm a great believer in turning up Hangmore Hill and going round by the pre-fabs on the Common.

RALPH: Yes yes, there's something to be said for that, too. What was the traffic like in Sudstow, then, John?

JOHN: Getting a bit sticky.

HOWARD: Yes, it was getting a bit sticky in Broylesden. How was it in Dorris Hill, Ralph?

RALPH: Sticky, pretty sticky.

MOTHER: The traffic's terrible round here now. There was a most frightful accident yesterday just outside when ...

HOWARD: Oh, you're bound to get them in traffic like this. Bound to.

RALPH: Where did you strike the traffic in Sudstow, then, John?

JOHN: At the lights by the railway bridge. Do you know where I mean?

RALPH: Just by that dance hall where they had the trouble?

JOHN: No, no. Next to the neon sign advertising mattresses.

HOWARD: Oh, you mean by the caravan depot? Just past Acme Motors?

JOHN: Acme Motors? You're getting mixed up with Heaslam Road, Surley.

HOWARD: I'm pretty sure I'm not, you know.

JOHN: I think you are, you know.

HOWARD: I don't think I am, you know.

JOHN: Anyway, that's where I struck the traffic.

RALPH: I had a strange experience the other day.

JOHN: Oh, really?

RALPH: I turned left at the lights in Broylesden High Street and cut down round the back of Coalpit Road. Thought I'd come out by the Wemblemore Palais. But what do you think happened? I came out by a new parade of shops, and I thought, hello, this must be Old Hangmore. Then I passed an Odeon —

JOHN: An Odeon? In Old Hangmore?

RALPH: — and I thought, that's strange, there's no Odeon in Old Hangmore. Do you know where I was? In New Hangmore!

HOWARD: Getting lost in New Hangmore's nothing. I got lost last week in Upsome!

JOHN: I went off somewhere into the blue only yesterday not a hundred yards from Sunnydeep Lane!

MOTHER: I remember I once got lost in the most curious circumstances in Singapore ...

RALPH: Anybody could get lost in Singapore, Mother.

JOHN: To become personal for a moment, Howard, how's your car?

HOWARD: Not so bad, thanks, not so bad. And yours?

JOHN: Not so bad, you know. How's yours, Ralph?

RALPH: Oh, not so bad, not so bad at all.

MOTHER: I had another of my turns last week.

HOWARD: We're talking about cars, Mother, CARS.

MOTHER: Oh, I'm sorry.

JOHN: To change the subject a bit — you know where Linden Green Lane comes out, just by Upsome Quadrant?

HOWARD: Where Tunstall Road joins the Crescent there?

RALPH: Just by the Nervous Diseases Hospital?

JOHN: That's right. Where the new roundabout's being built.

HOWARD: Almost opposite a truss shop with a giant model of a rupture belt outside?

RALPH: Just before you get to the bus station?

HOWARD: By the zebra crossing there?

JOHN: That's right. Well, I had a puncture there on Friday.

RALPH: Well, then, I suppose we ought to think about getting back.

HOWARD: I thought I might turn off by the paint factory on the by-pass this time and give the Apex roundabout a miss.

JOHN: Have either of you tried taking that side road at Tillotsons' Corner?

RALPH: There's a lot to be said for both ways. A lot to be said.

MOTHER: I'll go and make the tea while you discuss it, then. I know you've got more important things to do than sit here listening to an old woman like me chattering away all afternoon.

Fat Cat

Brett Roberts

The fat cat sat on the mat.

Correction; the fat cat sprawled on the spotless Wilton rug, warming his snow-white belly before the synthetic log-fire, stretching his well-groomed tabby limbs.

His name, absurdly, was Edward K. Pulvermacher, so called by Mr and Mrs Barry Harkup, 24 Dene Close, shortly after they had opened their front door to a wet, mewing kitten a year or two before and had taken it immediately to their childless bosoms.

Ed (for short) stirred in his dreams of poached mice on anchovy toast, awoke, arose, stretched both forelegs to an incredible length, meanwhile arching his elegant back.

Time for din-dins.

In a moment, he was in the kitchen, softly stropping his left flank, then his right, against the slim, nylon-clad ankles of Moira Harkup, who was half-way through preparing a *Gostolette di vitello alla Valdostama* for the evening meal.

The veal cutlets, half-stuffed with Fontina cheese and canned white truffles, had to wait while Moira minced Ed's fresh liver (it was Tuesday) and poured the top off a bottle of milk into a bowl simply inscribed 'His'.

Ed sat, curled his tail round his rump, and ate. You would think that a well-balanced fat cat, treated like the first-born son of a wealthy duke, would sit around and enjoy the luxury of life, twenty-four hours a day.

Not so. No sooner had the last shred of liver, the last whisker-drip of cream, disappeared into that delicate pink maw than Ed was at the kitchen door.

Moira looked at him, shaking her head sadly, 'Edward,' she said, 'aren't we doing enough for you? We give you a lovely home, haddock fillets, calves' liver, the top of the milk, my best brocade cushion to sleep on? What else, for heaven's sake?'

But Ed, as ever, had made his mind up. His schedule was immutable. 'Out!' he shouted over his shoulder. So out he went, as every evening after dinner, every morning after elevenses.

'Really!' said Moira, as Ed took off from the herb garden, scarcely touched the top of the six-foot fence, and disappeared with an insolent flick of his tail.

An hour or so later, the *Gostolette di Vitello* settled comfortably within, Barry and Moira decided to go along to the nearest Classic to see a film.

But they never got there, because Barry wanted a quick half-pint first, because the film finished after closing time. They made a brief detour towards the Lame Duck, but again they never got there because half-way along a short, narrow road called Pickens Court (former artisan cottages converted, at enormous expense, to bijou town houses), Barry stopped dead, grabbed Moira by the upper arm, and shouted, 'Great heavens, Moira, look!'

Moira looked towards a window back-lit by the discreet, orange lighting of somebody's through lounge. On the ledge inside the window sat a fat cat, tabby with white under-carriage.

'Am I seeing things,' asked Barry, 'or is that Ed?'

'It is Ed,' said Moira, simply, but with feeling. 'It could only be Ed.'

By this time Barry had his thumb firmly on an illuminated bell-push, and melodious chimes were repeating themselves faintly but urgently within.

'But Barry,' said Moira anxiously, 'what are you going to say?'

'Leave it to me,' said Barry. 'We shall have to play this thing by ear.'

The door opened, but not widely, and a thin man in very casual gear raised his eyebrows at them.

'Sorry to bother you,' said Barry, 'but the cat in the window ...'

'Not for sale,' said the thin man, bristling slightly.

'I should think not!' shouted Moira. 'It's our cat!'

'I beg your pardon,' said the thin man, bristling much more. 'That cat is Percy and he's definitely our cat ... And,' he began to close the door firmly, 'I wish you a very good evening.'

It was Moira's foot that got in the doorway first, though Barry's was beaten only by a short toe-cap.

The thin man, being a civilized citizen and realizing that the matter was serious, invited them in.

In a few moments the thin man and his wife (who was not thin) had introduced themselves as Arthur and Ruth Hellingly, and in a few moments more the Hellinglys and the Harkups were standing in an awkward, perplexed group looking at Edward, alias Percy, who was unconcernedly cleaning up.

'I do assure you,' said Moira, 'that this is definitely Edward, our cat.'

She groped in her handbag and produced a dog-eared colour snap of a fat cat, 'Look — that heart-shaped white patch on his shoulder ...'

Ruth Hellingly moved swiftly over to an Art Nouveau bureau.

She produced another, almost identical colour snap, showing the unmistakable heart-shaped white patch on the shoulder.

'Snap,' said Ruth triumphantly.

Crisis point. Clearly, Edward (or Percy) was leading a double life. 'We need,' said Arthur 'an independent referee. Somebody who can decide, impartially, whose cat this is.'

'Somebody like Mr Gorringe?' suggested his wife.

'Exactly,' said Arthur, and turned with an explanatory gesture to the Harkups. 'Mr Gorringe is a lawyer friend of ours. There will be no question of a fee. We know him well.'

'George Gorringe?' interrupted Barry. 'I know him, too — an excellent man. Judgement of Solomon and all that.'

'That sort of thing,' said Arthur. 'Might as well settle it now.' He reached for the telephone.

'Hello! That you, Gorringe? Hellingly here. Got a sort of legal problem we want to settle on the spot ... No, no. Nothing really legal. Just a little domestic matter that will appeal to your basic interest in jurisprudence ... Yes ... And I'm just opening a couple of bottles of Pouilly-Fuisse ... You'll come right away? Good !'

The first bottle was empty when George Gorringe rang the chimes and was admitted.

He joined the Harkups and the Hellinglys, standing round the hearth-rug, wine glasses in hand, at their feet a fat cat who was washing his nether fur with a long, pink tongue, his left leg hoisted skywards, so that he appeared to be playing a miniature cello.

Mr Gorringe looked at the cat, astonishment shining in his pale blue eyes. 'Fred!' he said. 'What the hell are you doing here?'

The List
of All Possible
Answers

Peter Goldsworthy

Peter Goldsworthy was born in South Australia in 1951. When asked how he
came to write 'The List of All Possible Answers' he replied, 'I'm a parent —
enough said'. Many of his stories are set in South Australia. They range from
the serious to the farcical in theme, and contain imagery that is both vivid and
original. His novels *Maestro* and *Honk If You Are Jesus* have both received
literary acclaim.

1

Again the child plucked at his mother's sleeve.

'Why do onions make my eyes water?' he demanded to know.
'Why?'

She shook her arm free and continued chopping the slippery, soapish
segments, trying to ignore him. But there was to be no escape.

'Mummy, Mummy — why do …'

At precisely that moment the idea came to her.

'Three,' she said.

'Three?'

'Three,' she repeated. 'The answer to your question is three.'

Silence descended while the child puzzled at this.

'What's three mean?' he shortly came out with.

'One of Mummy's little jokes,' his father, slicing tomatoes at the
other end of the bench, intervened. 'Another of Mummy's little jokes.'

He was not amused. But how else was she to cope? Battling away in a
classroom full of Year Fives all day, then home to this. A second classroom, she was beginning to think it. No, worse: a second front.

'The head is like a pressure-cooker,' she began to explain, speaking in
the direction of her son, but actually through him to his father. 'It can
only hold so much.'

She paused, averted her face from the onions momentarily, screwed up her eyes, then continued: 'If a joke doesn't emerge from the mouth, steam will shoot out the ears …'

'Or worse,' her husband added — also talking through the medium of their child. 'Or worse.'

'I still don't get it,' the boy said. 'What's number three?'

'Number three,' she told him. 'On the list.'

'What list?'

'I'll show you after dinner.'

'What's for dinner?'

She bit her tongue. These endless chains of question, response — once begun there was no ending them. From the moment she collected the child from creche to the moment he finally succumbed to sleep some hours later — this chatter ceasing suddenly, his neck muscles giving out, head plopping softly onto the plllow mid-sentence — he never stopped plucking sleeves, turning up that insistent face, repeating his endless interrogations. *Why, Mummy? Why? Why?*

'The list,' he remembered as he helped the two of them clear the table after dinner. 'The list! The list!'

'Yes, the list,' his father echoed, teasing her. 'Show us the list, Mummy!'

She retreated into the study, and tucked a sheet of quarto into the typewriter. The list took some time — it was little more than an idea, after all. And as for her typing — search and destroy, her husband liked to mock it.

The List of All Possible Answers, she typed across the head of the page, patiently seeking out each individual key, and destroying. That accomplished, she began to move down in a vertical column.

#1. No.

#2. Maybe.

#3…

Here she paused. Three? She was tired, the thoughts refused to flow … *Because*, she finally improvised, then removed her handiwork from the carriage and returned to the kitchen. As she taped the list to the fridge door, her husband peered over her shoulder.

'Because?' he wondered. 'What kind of answer is that? Because what?'

'Because nothing,' she said. 'Just because.'

'Sounds like a cop-out to me.'

'It's not a definitive list,' she defended herself. 'Feel free to add to it.'

He opened the fridge door, and unzipped a can of beer.

'Because that's the way God made it?' he suggested, sipping.

She laughed out loud: 'Who was accusing whom of a cop-out?'

She pulled open a kitchen drawer, scrabbled among the odds and ends, and emerged with a pen. *Because that's the way things are*, she added to the list, landing the full stop with a definitive thud.

'It's still a cop-out,' he insisted. He opened the fridge door and reached inside again. 'You want a beer?'

'Four,' she said.

'You want *four* beers?'

'The answer to your question is number four.'

He looked at the list. 'I don't see any number four.'

'Ask me tomorrow,' she yawned. 'I'm going to bed.'

2

She watched with interest as he fetched his first can from the fridge the next evening after work.

#4., he paused to read as he opened the door. *Ask me again tomorrow.*

'Your list of all answers,' he told her, 'is beginning to look like a list of all evasions.'

'Congratulations,' she said. 'You just caught on.'

The list grew quite quickly in the days that followed. #5. — *What do you think?* — was pencilled in the following night, and #6. — *Because I said so* — added the night after that. Towards the end of the week, however, the rate of increase seemed to slow. After #7. — *You're too young to understand* — there were no further additions for several days.

'Finished, have we?' her husband, who had been pretending to ignore it all, couldn't prevent himself asking. 'Finished our little joke?'

'No,' she said.

'How many more?'

She paused, considering.

'A finite number,' she guessed. 'Maybe ten. Yes, ten should just about cover everything.'

But there were loopholes still, she discovered.

'What's finite mean, Mummy?'

#8., she wrote. *Look it up in the Britannica.*

'What's the Britannica, Mummy?'

She scanned the seven preceding entries without reward.

'The answer to that could be nine,' her husband intervened — aid from an unexpected quarter.

'Nine?' the child wondered.

'Ask Mummy when she's in a better mood,' he smiled. 'Ask Mummy when she's learnt a little patience.'

He took a red felt-tip pen from the drawer and added the words in inch-high letters at the bottom of the list. *#9. ASK MUMMY WHEN SHE'S IN A BETTER MOOD.*

'Enough is enough,' he said. 'The joke has gone too far.'

3

The blank façade of the fridge struck him the moment he entered the kitchen the following night. Once again, she was watching carefully.

'Where's the list?' he asked.

'Where's the list?' their child, trotting behind, echoed.

'You were right,' she said. 'The joke had gone too far.'

Her husband smiled, but the child's lower lip began to tremble.

'I want my list,' he stammered. 'I want my answer list.'

'The list has gone,' his father bent to tell him. 'It was a silly list.'

But the child would not be comforted.

'No,' he shouted, twisting away. 'No! I want my list.'

As he ran from the room, his mother was already sifting through the kitchen waste-basket. She found the crumpled sheet, smoothed it between hand and bench, and began to tape it back onto the fridge.

'Please,' her husband said. 'No.'

'Yes,' she insisted.

'How much longer?'

'I don't know,' she admitted. 'I honestly don't know.'

He took a pen from his pocket.

#10., he wrote. *I don't know. I honestly don't know.*

He ruled a thick line across the page beneath his words. If nothing else, there would — surely — be no need for further entries.

Through the Wilderness   *Michael Frayn*

Discussion

1   Do you find this story funny? Give reasons for your response.

2   What sort of a person do you think the mother is in this story? How do you know?

3   *Satire* is a mixture of humour and criticism. The satirist wishes to entertain the reader, but also to make the reader aware of the vices or shortcomings of the subject. What is Michael Frayn satirising in this short short story?

Activities

1   Photocopy this short short story and then cut up the dialogue into individual speeches. Next, rearrange them, omitting some if necessary. Is your new version funnier than the original, and, if so, why?

2   During the family discussion, Mother begins to speak several times but always is interrupted. Choose one of her lines and imagine that she is allowed to continue speaking for a page. What does she say?

3   Choose a typical teenage topic, and use it to develop a dialogue along the lines of the one in 'Through the Wilderness'. Set it out in the same way.
      A group of girls might be talking about boys, fashion, music, films or sport, whilst a group of boys might be discussing sport, films, music, fashion or girls. Give it a clear satirical edge.

Fat Cat   *Brett Roberts*

Discussion

1   Do you find this story funny? Give reasons for your response.

2   What sort of a couple are the Harkups? How do you know?

3   The big laugh comes in the final line of this short short story, but are there any other amusing moments? Read the story again, looking for puns, irrelevant information, repetition and ironic human behaviour to help you with your answer.

Activities

1   Imagine that Ed/Percy/Fred can talk. (He has already 'spoken' one word in this story!) What might his reply be to Mr Gorringe's question in the last line of the story?

2   Imagine that the Harkups, the Hellinglys and the Gorringes decide to sell their cat. Devise an enthusiastic newspaper advertisement for Ed/Percy/Fred, but one which also includes a subtle warning about his behaviour which you can appreciate but which the new owner will not initially understand.

3 Look at the first line of 'Fat Cat'. Write a story of your own, beginning with a line from a children's nursery rhyme or early reader. Make your story as original and unpredictable as you can.

The List of All Possible Answers   *Peter Goldsworthy*

Discussion

1 Do you find this story funny? Give reasons for your response.

2 What is the relationship between the father and the mother in this story? What parts of the story give you the clues to this relationship? Comment on them in your answer.

3 What effect does the *layout of a story* have upon its readers? Look at the way this story has been set out on the page. Why are there so many paragraphs in this story? Why do you think the author has divided the story into three sections?

Activities

1 Imagine that you are your English teacher. Write a list of ten possible answers which will cover all the questions that you might ever be asked in class.

2 'Where's the list?' he asked.
'Where's the list?' their child, trotting behind, echoed.
  Mimicry is often amusing. When a writer copies the style of another author, playwright or poet etc. this is called *parody*. Try this yourself. Take a well-known children's story or nursery rhyme, and write it in the style of Virginia Andrews, Stephen King, Shakespeare, Jane Austen or any other writer that you know well. (You might also try writing it in the style of a government brochure, a television advertisement or a sports commentary.)

3 What makes a story funny? Humour is achieved in this story by contrasting the behaviour of mother and child, and showing someone behaving irrationally while under stress. One of the chief ingredients of humour is the use of the unexpected. A mood or story may be interrupted by a completely unexpected observation or activity. A person may behave in an unexpected way, for example, an adult may behave like a child. Anti-social behaviour is also amusing for the same reason. Write an amusing story. You may write about anything you like, but your purpose is to make your readers laugh.

The Pepper Tree

Wendy Stack

Wendy Stack was born in Australia in 1962, the daughter of Dutch immigrants. She has always been aware of the two cultures in her life. She writes, 'I left home and school early, giving up a planned higher education to live the way I believed'. She once lived on a farm where an old pepper tree grew, its presence providing her with comfort and inspiration.

I wait for Tim. I wait in the damp, cold room. I wait with the despairing ceiling and the yellow-stained walls. I wait with the patchwork bed-spread, Dale's paintings and the flowers. The flowers, picked one winter Sunday, now dead in the corner. The tiny dried blossoms fall to the floor and mingle with the dust. I wait with the pepper tree. Its green, delicately fringed leaves screen the window and keep away the blue, blue sky. I wait in the hushed light.

He doesn't come. I want to feel anger but there is no anger. Only fear. A small hungry fear that tightens in my stomach and creeps into my muscles. A tension coils in my body and has no escape. He doesn't want me. He has left me alone with the day. An empty stretch of time that I cannot fill. I stay in my cold room, afraid.

I am a failure. A nineteen-year-old failure. I have no job. I have no piece of paper to say I am educated. I have no money. I am not close to my family. I am insecure with my friends. I live in a house with a woman and her snivelling boy. The boy irritates me and the woman, who was once my closest friend, is no longer. I have no future. I have Tim.

I stay in my room and listen to Jackson's wailing — his monotonous crying broken by Karen yelling, Karen slapping, Karen crying, 'Leave me alone, shut up, shut up!' The television is on and the regional advertise-ments are repeated every ten minutes. No one goes out. They stay and wait in this awful neglected house. I no longer know what Karen and Jackson wait for or what they want. I wait for Tim.

I meet him on Highatt Street. It is late and we sit at a table in a shadowy coffee shop. He orders coffee and a walnut cake for himself. I don't want anything to eat. I want to appear self-controlled and disciplined but I am nervous. His green eyes put me on edge. I am frightened of being a fool, I am frightened of showing my feelings, I am frightened of failing in his eyes.

He says he is sorry and he holds my hand. Our conversation goes its usual way. Yes, things are mundane. Yes, I am still broke. Yes, Karen gives me the shits and, no, I haven't found a job. I haven't found a job. Those words are my shame, my embarrassment, my sense of self-worth sliding into the coffee. Tim is supportive, but then Tim has been employed all his working life. Varied jobs, interesting jobs. Tim has gotten every job he ever applied for. Tim believes there are jobs out there for people who really want to work. Tim has that easy confidence, that golden-haired, natural confidence. Tim is employable and I am not.

I take him home to my bedroom and the pepper tree. Stars are framed in its branches and there is moonlight on the leaves. The house is silent for us. There is no one to observe, no one to care. Tim holds my body with love and I have him. I have this confident, golden-haired man. I have his green eyes and his warm mouth. I have his strength. He makes my life all right.

On a wet, slick afternoon he arrives with a present. It is a cat, ginger and ugly. A half-wild female, it cringes in a corner of my room. It knocks over the dead flowers and slinks under the cupboard. Tim laughs and says she's a stray that wandered in at … work. His wife has had their second child. A boy. Golden-haired. The cat must be my consolation. I don't want it but I will love the cat because Tim gave it to me.

The cat is unfriendly. She will not purr. She slinks through the house and ignores the mice. I watch her, day after day, as she climbs the pepper tree and flattens herself to a branch. Eyes burning, body tense and pre-pared she waits for rosellas. I feed her extra but she continues to stalk birds.

Tim doesn't come round very often. He's busy. The new baby. I try to fill the endless afternoons. I pick some of the pepper tree berries. They are pink and papery and smell of pepper. I plant some and use others as decorations. The dead flowers and dust are swept up and the stoneware bowl is filled with the grapelike bunches.

Jackson is grizzling and I ask Karen if I can take him for a walk. He is happy in the pusher. We pick handfuls of the bare, curled branches of a tortured willow. I fill the pusher with branches and Jackson walks home, proud and useful, dragging two willow canes. Karen and I arrange the branches in large glass containers. We talk and laugh for the first time in months.

I wait for the pepper berries to sprout. I wait for them to grow. I join the library and my room is littered with gardening books. Books about trees and flowers, Books about life; green, growing life. The seedlings break the soil. They grow.

I think about Tim and read my books. I look at trees and know their names. Spotted gum, *eucalyptus maculata*. Pepper tree, *schinus molle*. I talk to wonderful old people, their gardens alive with flowers and creepers. I help an elderly lady dig up her overgrown bamboo clump and take home sacks of greenery. I spend afternoons potting up fuchsia and camellia cuttings, dividing geranium and daisy clumps, creating a plant nursery below the pepper tree. I walk through the Avenue of Honour with awakened senses and smell and touch the trees. Scarlet oaks, *Quercus coccinea*.

The pepper seedlings are four inches high and the cat is pregnant. For the first time, Tim makes a choice. He won't visit the house again. He won't lie on my velvet bed and watch rosellas or feel the damp night filter through the tree. He won't see the cold, starred skies. He won't hear my dreams, feel my fears, share my secrets. He won't have my love.

Jackson finds another dead rosella. Its head has been chewed off. Karen says it's that cat. It *is* that cat. That nearly feral cat. That ugly, pregnant cat. Tim's cat. I make a choice. Bluey Anderson comes over in the afternoon and shoots her cleanly. One careful, precise shot in the head. Jackson and I bury the cat under the pepper tree. It is hard going, digging a deep-enough hole between the roots. We do it.

Karen makes afternoon tea and we have it outside in the winter sunshine. Jackson drops his biscuit in the dirt, picks it up, puts it in his mouth and falls over in the wet grass. He gets up, laughing and spitting biscuit. It's a picnic, we say.

I transfer the pepper seedlings to individual pots. Eight die and two live. The cuttings have new leaves and the daisy flowers in a large yellow splash by the front door. Karen's mother buys two of my bamboo plants and I put my name down at McLintocks nursery. The librarian has told me about the T.A.F.E. courses. I sign up for horticulture and an external landscape gardening course.

On pension day I shop at Coles and choose a quality sketch-pad. I want to draw my gardens, put onto paper my designs, my creations. I buy lettuce and tomato plants and a packet of corn seeds. I see Tim pushing a laden trolley. He appears embarrassed, but he smiles and we try to talk. I tell him I'm busy, that I'm starting a vegetable garden. He wants to know about the cat. I say it's fine. He says he misses me. His wife waves and he pushes the trolley towards her. A wheel locks and he has to push it sideways. As I pay for my articles I can hear it clattering down the aisles.

I fantasize about Tim as I walk home. I think about his voice and his eyes and his hair. The pain hasn't gone. The emptiness is still there. I am a failure. I have nothing. No job, no money, no Tim.

I place the vegetable seedlings in my pepper tree nursery. The trestle-table is covered in potted greenery and there is an old-fashioned scent of geranium and columbine. A drift of pepper and hope is in the air.

I am a gardener. I have a future. I have myself.

The Hairpiece

NA Hilton

The guardian angel sighed as she looked at Soul/Earth/19664/MG.

She should be used to it by now but it still hurt. She raised her arm and the Disposal Cherub began to materialize in a rosy glow beside her ...

Everything was quiet, as usual, in the convent high in the Italian hills, Sister Benedict prayed happily, absorbed as usual in her one-sided, but satisfying conversation with Our Lady.

The birds sang and the sun shone but the little Sister heard nothing of the world outside.

Reverend Mother had been right to rebuke her; her mind had wandered during evening meal yesterday, while Sister Mary was reading from the *Life of Saint Teresa*. However, penance had been done, and it would not happen again ...

In her London flat, Julia sat and looked at herself in the dressing-table mirror. Not too bad, everything considered. Thank God it was all cut and dried now, all arrangements made.

She looked at her watch — 10.30. The taxi should be here in fifteen minutes. Time for the finishing touches. No crawling there looking like a wreck, she was going to march into that clinic with her head held high and looking her very best.

Why had she hesitated so long? She had written three times to Alan, the first time a gay, chatty letter asking him about the tour, asking how the Americans liked the British orchestras, and how she missed him.

She wasn't really surprised to receive no reply to her letter. Travelling around from town to town on a concert tour would take a little time to catch up with him.

Next time she wrote she was sure about the baby, but said nothing, only how were things over there, and she missed him …missed him.

The third letter had been very hard to write. The version she finally sent said, 'Darling, guess what? We're going to have a baby, isn't it a mad thing to happen? No regrets darling, only write if you want to. Love Julia.'

She hadn't really expected a reply, and she didn't receive one.

Of course, she could not look after a baby alone so she made a phone call to Cynthia, she scribbled down a telephone number, collected her savings from the Post Office, and made an appointment for today at a discreet clinic. She looked at her watch; just half an hour.

Three days, all over, no baby, no Alan.

She looked again in the mirror, nearly ready, nails done, false eye-lashes helping to hide the dark shadows under her eyes; hair brushed back, ready for the finishing touch.

She lifted the hairpiece out of its box, lovely long silky hair, pale gold, coiled into a neat twist, and pinned it carefully into place.

The thought struck her like a slap in the face, like icy fingers squeezing her very being. 'Can't do it … I can't … my baby, no they shall not.'

The face staring back at her in the mirror was deathly white, the black-circled eyes shrunken. Oh God, she thought, I look like a clown. She started to laugh quietly, then biting her lip and shaking, 'Stop it, stop it, you fool,' she said aloud.

No food, that was it, no breakfast.

She looked at her watch again, just time for coffee and toast. She made sure the varnish was dry on her nails, put the hairpiece carefully back in its box and went into the tiny kitchenette of the flat. She put the coffee on to perk, and felt better.

Of course she was doing the right thing, whatever had caused that absurd moment of doubt earlier, everything was quite clear now in her mind.

She drank the coffee, nibbled the toast and went back to finish getting ready. Now … handbag ready, yes, suitcase for three days, yes, note for the milkman. She lifted the hairpiece from its box, pinned it into place, and heard the taxi draw up outside.

This time the clarity of the sudden realization of what she was going to do hit her mind with such force that it was all she could do not to fall off the chair.

She gripped the dressing table with both hands while great sobs wracked her body. There was a knock on the door, 'Taxi, madam.' No, no, go away. Shocked silence.

'Are you all right, madam?'

She pulled herself together and went to the door. 'Sorry, plans changed.' She thrust some money into his hand and shut the door, then sank down on the floor, sobbing quietly, almost happily.

We'll manage, she thought, my baby and I. We'll manage, somehow. She must have slept there on the floor till she woke with a bell ringing, urgently.

It took a few seconds to gather herself together and open the door. She stared stupidly at a small boy in a postman's uniform. 'Telegram, miss.'

She opened it and read, 'Coach in accident. Don't worry. All well, darling. Letters just reached me. Marry me next week. Look after yourself and our offspring. Love always, Alan.' Now she was really crying, but this time they were tears of pure joy ...

The Guardian Angel paused, a rare smile on her face. Gently, she lowered Soul/Earth/19664/MG back into the rosy cloudiness where he would stay for six more months, and before she turned away she put back the label on his incubator. Male/Ist class/genius/music ...

In the Italian convent the birds had gone to roost, the candles flickered as little Sister Benedict rose stiffly from her knees. She was deeply ashamed of herself. It had happened again — her thoughts had strayed. It was unforgivable, to think about herself.

It was just personal vanity to wonder what had become of the long pale gold hair she had so willingly allowed them to cut when she gave herself to God for ever. How could she think such dreadful thoughts when she was supposed to be praying for the souls of all unwanted children?

The Headache

Ann Hunter

As she lifted the shopping bag off the hall floor it dripped blood. Dull red on the polished parquet, it plopped steadily, so that Joanna stood transfixed, remembering.

'What on earth ... of course, it must be the liver. How stupid of me ...'

She rushed across the hall through the dining room, leaving the telltale stains like a paper-chase, and finally heaved the bag into the sink where it could drip without spoiling anything.

'Now where's the floorcloth ... Mrs Renwick's always rearranging these cupboard ... I must tell her not to ... Will blood stain the carpet? What should I use? Cold water first, I think.'

It was soon under control. Wiping the blood off the parquet flooring was easy, but seeing it there, that small puddle, she remembered ...

Joanna Nicholls prided herself on her beef stroganoff. It was her speciality. When guests came who had already sampled its delights, they begged for a second performance; those who hadn't, wished to be initiated. And so Joanna cooked vast quantities, ladled it into polythene containers and froze it in the 'gynormous' chest freezer in the back of the second garage. James had recently learnt this new word at school, and used it to describe anything bigger than himself.

Tonight the guests were important. Charles needed a loan — a big one — for extensions to the surgery. The bank manager and his wife, plus one of the senior partners and his wife were coming, ostensibly for a splendid stroganoff, in reality for business negotiations. Joanna sighed, pushing back the damp tendrils of hair from her forehead as she tasted the sauce.

'I don't find freezing it makes it stronger; it needs more pepper in it.'

'The table's finished.'

'Oh, thanks. You can pop off now if you want, Mrs Renwick. There's not much else to do. And thanks for doing such a lovely job with the flowers. See you Thursday.'

Mrs Renwick always looked so plump and healthy. The epitome of good nature ... how could she seem so happy, so relaxed, with that minute house, those awful children, no car, no money ...

'See you Thursday then. Hope you have a nice evening.'

Nice? No, it'll be the usual hell of putting on a brave face ... and being bored to tears.

Joanna replaced the heavy pot in the oven and went over to the mirror. She felt she still looked attractive, but there was no doubt that she was a mature woman. The wrinkles — laughlines Charles called them — round her eyes were very definite now, but her hair was still lovely. Soft curls, brown and silky — always gave her an Edwardian look when she wore her hair up — like tonight. She fussed briefly with the ruffles of her white blouse, arranging the locket so that it lay smoothly on the frothy lace cravat, then walked slowly into the lounge.

Charles sprawled on the sofa reading the *Lancet*. He didn't look up.

If only he'd talk to me now, before they all come. Treat me like a human being and not a piece of furniture ... or a T.V. only switched on when being looked at.

'Had a busy day?'

'Mm. Yes. Usual. Everything ready?'

'Yes. Fine. Like a drink?'

'No, I've already got one, thanks.'

And me. What about me? Or do I have to get my own?

Joanna went to the drinks cupboard and poured a gin — a big gin with very little tonic. The ice clinked comfortingly in the glass and she inhaled the heady perfume before taking a first tingling sip. All so peaceful. So ordinary. James. I haven't said goodnight to him.

'Have you said goodnight to James?'

'No — give him a kiss for me will you, Jo.'

Again. Always give him a hug — a kiss — from me. How can you be so lazy with your own son?

As she straightened the duvet and smoothed the schoolshirt hanging on the chair, she heard the door bell.

'See you tomorrow, Mum.'

'Yes. Goodnight, love, sleep tight.'

Loud murmurings from the hall, and hearty laughter. Joanna leaned against the cool tiles in the bathroom and breathed in her own rich perfume. Her body still glowed from her early evening bath; she felt fragrant, fresh. I wish I could stay up here with my son, or alone, and quietly read away the evening.

'Jo — they're here.'

'Coming.'

The cigar smoke curled upwards past the deep browns of the Laura Ashley curtains and hung in swathes around the dimmed lights.

'That was delightful, Joanna. You really are an excellent cook. You're a lucky man, Charles.'

Brian exhaled bonhomie with his cigar and looked sleek, satisfied. Just ripe for the plucking — Charles would get his loan. Harriet's quiet tonight though. I must get a chance to talk to her.

'You all right now, Joanna? After that nasty knock. Just shows you how easily accidents can happen.'

'I'm fine thanks, Geoffrey. Perfectly recovered.'

'You slipped, didn't you? On the *Lancet* of all things?'

'Yes, I'm always telling James not to dash around the house without his slippers on, and I ... well I was just off to bed, no shoes on, just stocking feet, and — of course I couldn't save myself. My arms were full of books and magazines actually, but even if they hadn't been, there was nothing I could do. My feet just shot from under me and wham ... straight on to that dresser. My uncle said it was solid oak when he gave it to us — now I can believe it.'

'And how long were you in hospital?'

'Only two days, you know. After they'd X-rayed my skull and given me the all clear. But it took me more than a week to get over it, I couldn't see straight, couldn't read, couldn't ...'

Charles stood up. 'Well, it's been most satisfactory to get things sorted out, hasn't it?'

'I quite agree.' Brian, like the others, took the hint and got up.

'No problems at all as far as we're concerned. A good investment for you is a good investment for us. You can count on us to put you right.'

As the last car drove out of earshot, Joanna emptied the ashtrays and straightened the cushions. Charles took her by the arm.

'Does it still bother you? Your head I mean?'

'Only sometimes. When it's damp I still get a twinge, a bit of a headache.'

'It won't happen again, you know, Jo. I promise you it won't happen again. I know I've got an awful temper, but it won't happen again.'

Until the next time. And who can a doctor's wife turn to? They don't have fitted carpets at Women's Aid, or gin ...

As she switched off the light in the hall, Joanna again remembered the blood, her blood on the parquet floor ...

'Please get the ambulance. For God's sake, Charles. I won't tell them. I'll say I slipped ... but for pity's sake... get the ambulance.'

I wonder if his other patients have to plead with him when they need to go to hospital.

'Do you want to read?'

'No thanks. I'll go straight to sleep tonight. Early clinic tomorrow. You all right?'

'Yes, fine thanks. I've just got a bit of a headache.'

Charles twisted towards her, laid his arm on hers. 'It makes me feel guilty. You know I never mean to harm you. If we could just try a bit harder ... if we ...'

'I'm tired, Charles. Goodnight.'

I never could understand women who stayed with men who hit them. I still can't.

The Pepper Tree   *Wendy Stack*

Discussion

1   Who or what was responsible for the change in the speaker during the course of this short short story?

2   Why do you think Tim was attracted to the owner of the pepper tree?

3   A *symbol* is a picture, an object or a sign which stands for something else. A snake, for example, has always symbolised evil. A symbol can stand for a message, an event or an abstract idea.
    a   How does the cat work as a symbol in 'The Pepper Tree'? What useful purpose is served by her presence in the story?
    b   Discuss any other symbols in this story.

Activities

1   In pairs, write and then perform the brief scene in which the speaker meets Tim in Coles supermarket. What is each person feeling? Try to capture the mood of the occasion.

2   Does this story have anything important to reveal to us about women's problems in today's society? Write a page in answer to this question, giving reasons for your point of view.

3   Write a story of your own in which a young person experiences a moment of self-knowledge. Here are three suggestions.
    A teenager realises that he or she:
    *   is responsible for someone else's unhappiness
    *   must stand alone
    *   is able to cope in a difficult situation.

The Hairpiece   *NA Hilton*

Discussion

1   Explain clearly the relationship that existed between the Guardian Angel, Sister Benedict and Julia.

2   How did you feel when you first read the section where Julia paid the taxi driver and decided to keep the baby? Give reasons for your response.

3   *Irony* exists when the outcome of a situation turns out to be the opposite (contrary) of what was expected. Explain the author's use of irony in 'The Hairpiece'.

Activities

1   At the finish of this short short story, Sister Benedict was supposed to be praying, but her thoughts were straying. Begin: 'Holy Mary, Mother of God …' and continue with the words that went through her head.

2   Record the conversation that took place between the Guardian Angel and the Disposal Cherub as they waited for Julia to prepare herself for the clinic. Conclude the conversation at the point when the taxi arrived.

3   If this story is a little unusual, it is because three separate worlds (an Italian convent, a London flat, and the Department of Souls in heaven) have been introduced to us with no initial explanation as to why they are there. Their connection is only revealed at the end of the story. Try a story of your own using this formula. Make your connections logical but not predictable. As with all storytelling, the reader should never be able to forsee the ending in advance.

The Headache   *Ann Hunter*

Discussion

1   Why did Charles hit Joanna? Why did Joanna stay with Charles?

2   What kind of a relationship did the Nicholls have? Would you say that Joanna Nicholls was a weak woman?

3   *Foreshadowing* is a writing technique an author uses to give an 'early echo' of some idea or event that will assume an importance later in the story. How does Ann Hunter use foreshadowing in 'The Headache'?

Activities

1   A local newspaper gets hold of the story of Charles hitting his wife. There is only space for fifty words (including the headline). Write the article.

2   In pairs, write and then perform the scene which ended with Charles hitting his wife. Decide upon their topic of argument, and build up the tension slowly. Finish with Joanna's line (spoken from the floor): 'Please get the ambulance. For God's sake, Charles …'.

3   Of course, women's concerns are men's concerns too. A good short short story, however, can make the reader more aware of some of the problems of our society. The stories must be written with an imaginative eye and a degree of honesty. Try writing one. Here are three suggestions.
   • A mother becomes aware that her child is a thief (or a bully, a drunkard etc.)
   • A child learns a truth about something one of his/her parents did before marriage.
   • Someone is forced to face the fact that they have AIDS.

The Colonial Girl

Betty Roberts

Betty Roberts was brought up in England, and spent many years in Kenya before finally settling with her family in Tasmania in the early 1960s. She now runs a small farm with her husband. Betty has been writing since her early teens, and her stories for both adults and children have appeared in many publications around the world. She is also an artist and poet.

I've heard it said that Jane was born in the wrong continent, or the wrong century ... perhaps both. I've known Jane — loved her too — ever since we met at matric college. Sometimes I wish we had never been contemporaries.

She was beautiful. Her lovely face wasn't the face of the 80's, however. It was a nineteenth-century face, glowing with life and yet calm and serene at the same time.

If you feel that's a silly remark to make — 'How can faces alter with the centuries?' — just think about some of the period programmes you've seen on television. There are men and women who look as though they have stepped out of an old picture frame, historical portraits suddenly warm and alive. That's how it was with Jane.

Her slim neck and lovely shoulders were never meant to be lost in layers of coarse knit sweaters nor disguised in unisex blue denim. She wore these things but somehow she gave the impression of being in costume — dressing the part of the twentieth-century girl.

Her serenity stood her in good stead at uni. So many girls seemed to be emotionally insecure. Not so Jane. Her graceful figure never appeared in any counsellor's office.

Some of her tutors found Jane's work slightly uncomfortable. She'd always had a tremendous interest in Tasmania's history. She was so sure of her subject, had such empathy with people long ago, that at times it seemed as though the shrewd and bookish Lady Franklin had returned to Hobart Town.

I was at art school and I still saw quite a lot of Jane. I was encouraged by the fact that she had no steady boyfriends. There was no shortage of escorts for parties and college functions; but Jane seemed to be looking for someone special, and unlike most of her fellow students she was prepared to wait.

Her parents, naturally enough, were proud of her academic success and delighted by her beauty. Her mother, I could tell, was keenly alert for any whisper of a young man who could match her darling girl.

Tall and handsome, of course, to complement Jane's dainty grace; wealthy, to surround her with the mellow beauty which meant more to her than the most gadget-filled modern home. And with a mind as quick and cultured as Jane's own — I could imagine the mother asking herself 'Do young men come like that any more?' I doubt if she even considered me as a possible son-in-law.

Then came Jane's twenty-first birthday. The party was arranged in one of Tasmania's historic country homes. Guests were asked to dress in suitably period costume for a colonial dinner in Jane's honour.

Electric sewing machines hummed as eager guests quickly duplicated the laborious handstitching of forgotten seamstresses. The theatrical companies did good business in hiring out costumes for the party. I decided on a naval uniform. I felt that this birthday dinner was going to be a crucial night in my relationship with Jane, and a well-fitting uniform has often proved an ally for the desperate suitor.

When Jane came into the panelled dining room that night we saw her as she was meant to be. I knew she was making her own costume and that it was to be a surprise. The dress was crisp and rustling in a subtle dark green colour. It had bands of a softer green on high puff sleeves and round the hem of the spreading skirt. My artist's observant eye subconsciously registered all this for future remembrance; at the time I was overwhelmed by Jane's utter perfection.

Her beautiful throat was circled by an antique necklace and matching drops hung from her ears. Her dark hair was dressed high with a deep fringe falling to her eyes. Jane belonged to her surroundings as never before and she seemed to move in a magical light all her own.

I enjoyed several dances with her but I felt I should not monopolize her on this special occasion. I watched as she circled the ballroom with a tall young fellow dressed in drab convict garb. Soldiers and bushrangers came in twos and threes, but the arrowed costume stood alone.

Jane whirled through several waltzes with this partner. I hated him on sight. When I saw them move to Jane's parents I too moved to stand nearby. I had to know who he was.

'Mother — father — may I present Charles Fenton?' Jane's formality was matched by the young man's graceful bow.

'Charles is from Essex in England,' I heard Jane say.

'You are visiting Tasmania?' her mother asked.

'Yes — I've been here for a while,' the young man smiled. He turned to Jane. 'And I hope to stay much longer.'

It happens so often to our local girls. They are whisked off by some chap from the mainland or overseas. Well, Charles Fenton was in for some strong competition from me.

They returned to the waltz. I overheard Jane's mother murmuring to her husband '*What* a nice young man! He's *right* for Jane, I know it!'

Jane's father shrugged. 'Bit of a snap decision, my dear?'

'But just *look* at them! I wonder who he's visiting?' Charles was looking down at Jane with obvious enchantment, while she smiled up at him. Her previous air of expectancy was replaced by an expression of rapt delight.

Jane's mother went on, 'I must ask around, find out where he's staying … but there, we shall be seeing him again, I'm sure.'

I mentally agreed with her, but the prospect didn't give me any pleasure. As it happened, we were both wrong. No one has seen Charles Fenton nor Jane since that night of the colonial dinner.

The police checked airports and ferry services. I drove hundreds of kilometres spurred by my own horrible hunches, searching quiet picnic areas and bushland trails I'd walked with Jane. No clues, no discovery, nothing.

Until yesterday. Glancing through a new book of early colonial drawings I saw a charcoal sketch of a young man's face which was faintly familiar. Where had I seen him — or someone like him?

The notes on the artist told me. She was the daughter of the original owner of the mansion where Jane had danced and disappeared. The sketch was of Charles Fenton, a transported forger who had worked on the building.

I drove out of town dangerously fast. None of us had looked in the tiny graveyard in the grounds of the old house. I found the stone, weatherworn and tipped sideways in the rich soil. The name 'Charles Fenton' was still legible. I could just make out part of the words 'convict' and 'Essex' lower on the stone.

Christmas
Meeting

Rosemary Timperley

Rosemary Timperley was born in 1920 in England, where she has become one of the country's most prolific and best loved writers of ghost stories. 'Christmas Meeting' was her first story, and her later pieces, like 'Christmas Meeting', generally feature gentle ghosts of the non-threatening variety. Her stories have not been collected together in book form.

I have never spent Christmas alone before.

It gives me an uncanny feeling, sitting alone in my 'furnished room', with my head full of ghosts, and the room full of voices of the past. It's a drowning feeling — all the Christmases of the past coming back in a mad jumble: the childish Christmas, with a house full of relations, a tree in the window, sixpences in the pudding, and the delicious, crinkly stocking in the dark morning: the adolescent Christmas, with mother and father, the war and the bitter cold, and the letters from abroad: the first really grown-up Christmas, with a lover — the snow and the enchantment, red wine and kisses, and the walk in the dark before midnight, with the grounds so white, and the stars diamond bright in a black sky — so many Christmases through the years.

And, now, the first Christmas alone.

But not quite loneliness. A feeling of companionship with all the other people who are spending Christmas alone — millions of them — past and present. A feeling that, if I close my eyes, there will be no past or future, only an endless present which is time, because it is all we ever have.

Yes, however cynical you are, however irreligious, it makes you feel queer to be alone at Christmas time.

So I'm absurdly relieved when the young man walks in. There's nothing romantic about it — I'm a woman of nearly fifty, a spinster school ma'am with grim, dark hair, and myopic eyes that once were beautiful, and he's a kid of twenty, rather unconventionally dressed with a flowing, wine-coloured tie and black velvet jacket, and brown curls which could do with a taste of the barber's scissors. The effeminacy of his dress is belied by his features — narrow, piercing, blue eyes, and arrogant, jutting nose and chin. Not that he looks strong. The skin is fine-drawn over the prominent features, and he is very white.

He bursts in without knocking, then pauses, says: 'I'm so sorry, I thought this was my room.' He begins to go out, then hesitates and says: 'Are you alone?'

' Yes.'

'It's — queer, being alone at Christmas, isn't it? May I stay and talk?'

'I'd be glad if you would.'

He comes right in, and sits down by the fire.

'I hope you don't think I came in here on purpose. I really did think it was my room,' he explains.

'I'm glad you made the mistake. But you're a very young person to be alone at Christmas time.'

'I wouldn't go back to the country to my family. It would hold up my work. I'm a writer.'

'I see.' I can't help smiling a little. That explains his rather unusual dress. And he takes himself so seriously, this young man! 'Of course, you mustn't waste a precious moment of writing,' I say with a twinkle.

'No, not a moment! That's what my family won't see. They don't appreciate urgency.'

'Families are never appreciative of the artistic nature.'

'No, they aren't,' he agrees seriously.

'What are you writing?'

'Poetry and a diary combined. It's called *My Poems and I,* by Francis Randel. That's my name. My family say there's no point in my writing, that I'm too young. But I don't feel young. Sometimes I feel like an old man, with too much to do before he dies.'

'Revolving faster and faster on the wheel of creativeness.'

'Yes! Yes, exactly! You understand! You must read my work some time. Please read my work! Read my work!' A note of desperation in his voice, a look of fear in his eyes, makes me say:

'We're both getting much too solemn for Christmas Day. I'm going to make you some coffee. And I have a plum cake.'

I move about, clattering cups, spooning coffee into my percolator. But I must have offended him, for, when I look round, I find he has left me. I am absurdly disappointed.

I finish making coffee, however, then turn to the bookshelf in the room. It is piled high with volumes, for which the landlady has apologized profusely: 'Hope you don't mind the books, Miss, but my husband won't part with them, and there's nowhere else to put them. We charge a bit less for the room for that reason.'

'I don't mind,' I said. 'Books are good friends.'

But these aren't very friendly-looking books. I take one at random. Or does some strange fate guide my hand?

Sipping my coffee, inhaling my cigarette smoke. I begin to read the battered little book, published, I see, in Spring, 1851. It's mainly poetry — immature stuff, but vivid. Then there's a kind of diary. More realistic, less affected. Out of curiosity, to see if there are any amusing comparisons, I turn to the entry for Christmas Day, 1851. I read:

'My first Christmas Day alone. I had rather an odd experience. When I went back to my lodgings after a walk, there was a middle-aged woman in my room. I thought, at first, I'd walked into the wrong room, but this was not so, and later, after a pleasant talk, she — disappeared. I suppose she was a ghost. But I wasn't frightened. I liked her. But I do not feel well tonight. Not at all well. I have never felt ill at Christmas before.'

A publisher's note followed the last entry: FRANCIS RANDEL DIED FROM A SUDDEN HEART ATTACK ON THE NIGHT OF CHRISTMAS DAY, 1851. THE WOMAN MENTIONED IN THIS FINAL ENTRY IN HIS DIARY WAS THE LAST PERSON TO SEE HIM ALIVE. IN SPITE OF REQUESTS FOR HER TO COME FORWARD, SHE NEVER DID SO. HER IDENTITY REMAINS A MYSTERY.

The Return

Marjory E Lambe

Marjory E Lambe was a pseudonym used by Gladys Gordon Trenery, born in 1885. She was a leading practitioner of the ghost story between the wars. She also wrote stories of the occult, but her pieces have never been collected together in book form. She died in 1938.

A night that was wild with wind and pitiless rain. Wind that tore at hair and clothing with gusty, bitter fingers; rain that lashed and drove and whimpered, like the sound of that croaking voice that had been stilled two years ago.

How he had whimpered, that old man! Surprised in the act of returning his ill-gotten gains to their stronghold, he who had always been so poor that he could not afford a living wage for his servants, nor an education for his son. Caught out, with his wealth around him to prove his lies!

The man who was tramping back towards the gloomy house in its nest of trees set his jaw in sullen, grim determination. For two years had that wealth lain there, useless and yet safe from prying eyes.

He alone, whose hand had struck him down, knew the secret of its hiding-place, and now that suspicion had died down and the law was quiet — aye, as quiet as that thing that lay in the churchyard yonder- he could come back and search for his rightful treasure in peace.

Rightful, did you say? Why, to be sure there was the old man's son, but his image was faint and shadowy in the mind of his father's murderer. Murder! How the word clung! The very trees seemed to whisper it as he passed. An ugly word, for an ugly thing.

It was not a nice thought, even now, to enter that shuttered house far away from the village, to force his way into the great gloomy room where that old man had whimpered before the look of horror in his eyes had turned to astonishment, and then — blind fear.

He drew his hat down over his eyes and plodded on, his hands buried deep in his pockets, and the sound of his heavy boots muffled in the soft mud until they were drowned altogether in the wind.

A dark bend in the road and the lights of the village shone out, blurred with rain. Recognition, he told himself, was impossible, and yet as he drew near the cheerful doorway of the 'White Horse' he hesitated.

Bodily fatigue and nervous strain combined in a craving for a draught of burning spirits — a draught that would cheer him and help to still that voice that cried at him in the darkness. Besides, he had thought a moment ago that he had seen an old white face peering at him from behind a tree-trunk in the hedge. Such fancies must be drowned and quickly, too.

After all, it was two years. There had never been more than two servants up at the house; himself and Benjamin Strong, the gardener. When he had fled the country the old man had been nearly as old as his master; it was ten chances to one that he was dead, too, by now. He had no one else to fear, therefore, except the son, and him he dismissed with a contemptuous shrug of his shoulders.

A shadow all his life, obsequious to the slightest whim of the old man, he would have left the neighbourhood long ago. He could not have kept up that great house on one hundred a year, which was all that his father had left him.

Once more he congratulated himself on the cunning that had induced him to move the body aside and hastily pack away the money into its hiding-place. Even if the house had been sold it would still be there. No one knew of it save himself. He was the only living soul who knew of its existence.

Exultation rose strong again in his breast, and he pushed open the door of the bar and entered.

Across the haze of tobacco smoke he seemed to hear his own voice asking for brandy, neat, and there was a ring in it that was unlike himself. He smiled as he tossed off the spirit, and asked for more.

He did not know that the girl looked at him strangely, he did not notice that the conversation in the room had ceased at his entrance, and that staring eyes were directed curiously towards him. But he did know that the girl took up his money and tossed it carelessly into an open drawer, and he knew that the tobacco smoke had wreathed itself into an old, avaricious face, bending low over it and looking up cunningly at him with a smile of triumph.

'Must have followed me in,' he muttered, and drew his hand over his eyes. It went then, vanished as suddenly as it had come, and he found that the girl was looking at him with frightened eyes.

'D'you want any change?' she asked, and then as he did not seem to understand, repeated in a louder voice: 'Any change?'

He tried to control his shaking voice, tried to speak distinctly.

'No,' he said. 'No. No change at all. He is just the same. Tell me,' he added, bending forward eagerly and laying a hot, dry hand on her arm, 'is he always like that? Does he still look at you and then at the money?'

She shook off his hand.

'Get along with you,' she said disgustedly. 'I thought you were ill. You are only drunk.' But her eyes were watching him closely and she was trying to see the expression of his face beneath the low brim of his hat.

He felt furiously indignant.

'Never been drunk in my life,' he assured her. 'Never. Always a steady character. Always.'

'Well, you are unsteady enough tonight,' she told him partly over her shoulder as she turned away, and a general laugh made him aware that he had attracted considerable attention, and that in spite of her seeming indifference she was regarding him curiously. Fear, returning swiftly, whispered of recognition, and with a muttered curse he thrust his shaking hands into his pockets and went out.

As the door swung to behind him a man stepped up to go in and the light fell full on his face. He was old, but he was still upright, and the face, though wrinkled, was full of health and vigour. The man in the shadows stepped back quickly into the darkness, and although the other did not glance in his direction, it was some moments before he could control his nerves sufficiently to go on. For the man who had passed him was Benjamin Strong.

Alone once more, he fumbled for his handkerchief and wiped away the sweat that had started to his face. Then he pulled himself together as far as his ragged nerves would permit and started on the last lap of his journey.

The house was not far now. Two turnings and a stretch of dark lane brought him to a gate, gleaming white in the darkness.

His fingers were some time unfastening it, although it was only latched, but it swung open at last with a grating against the gravel. As he made his way up the long, grass-grown avenue he told himself that the wind had risen. How it roared in the bare branches above his head, now rising to a scream as if it were an old voice screaming in that last cry for mercy, now dying away to a whisper —

The click of the gate behind him made him start. He had left it open. Had it shut of its own accord, or was it because someone had brushed it in passing through?

He breathed a sigh of relief when the house loomed up before him. It was evidently still empty, for the windows were shuttered and they had boarded up that little window at the side, but the boards were insecurely fastened, and a pocket-knife and hasty fingers quickly removed them.

A cracked voice muttering:

'That's the way in,' made him sweat with fear until he realised that it was himself.

It was better inside the house than in the gusty avenue, with the wind full of strange sounds. He had thought he had heard a footstep on the gravel a moment ago, a slow slouching footstep, like that of an old man —

Matches refused to light when struck by trembling fingers, but he knew his way so well that he could grope along by the wall as far as the stairs. Each board creaked as he mounted, and halfway up he stopped short, shaking, for a door had slammed somewhere in the distance. He waited for five gasping seconds, but no further sound reached him except the wind in the trees, and cursing himself for a frightened fool, he stumbled on.

But his limbs were trembling and his hands were clammy with sweat.

He reached the room at last, and had used up all his matches before he remembered his electric-torch.

The furniture remained the same as it had been that night. The chairs were pushed back, the tablecloth was dragged half off the table and the very vase of flowers that he had knocked over in the struggle was smashed on the floor with the dry dead flowers scattered in all directions.

'Dead,' he muttered aloud, and grew weirdly, horribly afraid.

The spring by the fireplace was stiff with disuse, but it worked at last, and his fears momentarily vanished as he bent over the secret drawer. Eager fingers groped their way into the dim recess, and at last, with a gasp of trembling joy, he drew out roll after roll of notes, bag after bag of coins.

'Hundreds of pounds!' he croaked. 'Hundreds! And all mine! Hundreds of —'

And then stopped quite suddenly, the words frozen on his lips.

Only the creaking of a board, that was all, but he knew as well as if he could see it, that that shuffling footstep had followed him from the avenue, through the window and up the stairs. He could hear it coming slowly down the corridor.

With a sobbing gasp he flashed his torch upon the slowly opening door,and as the white arc of light lit up the open space he saw that grinning wizened face looking in at him.

The white hair was streaked with blood, the skin was yellow across the skeleton face, but the bloodless lips were drawn back in a grin of pure triumph.

The old man had come back to guard his treasure, and suddenly his wretched victim knew that he had not come for the money. That was only the bait that had set the trap —

The shuffling footsteps came nearer, and with them the grinning face, and then it was that something snapped in his brain. A wild scream rang through the silent house, the torch dropped to the ground, and he pitched forward into a darkness that seemed to hold the mocking laughter of fiends.

'What shall we do with him, sir?'

The old man's son threw a contemptuous glance at the prostrate figure at his feet.

'You'd better take him away, Inspector. Hold the candle nearer. Isn't dead, is he?'

'No, sir. A fit, I should say.'

'Poor devil. He's been punished enough already. As for me, I don't care what you do with him. He showed me the way to the secret hiding-place, and that was all that I wanted.'

He turned to a white-faced girl who was standing behind him.

'And you deserve half the spoils, Bessie, for spotting him.'

She shivered slightly.

'I wasn't alone, sir. There wasn't a man in the bar that didn't spot him, too, and it only wanted Benjamin Strong to settle it.' She shivered again and glanced over her shoulder into the shadows. 'Wonder what he thought he saw, sir, when you pushed open the door?'

The old man's son laughed.

'Nerves, my dear,' he said, 'and a guilty conscience, that's all.'

But his laughter did not ring quite true and his eyes followed hers into the shadows beyond the door, for he fancied he had heard a low, wicked chuckle by the stairs. He stepped to the doorway and listened, and was it only a rat in the walls or did a shuffling footstep pass on down to the empty hall?

Returning quicky to the dimly-lit room, he was met by the Inspector. 'I made a mistake, sir,' he said. 'The man is dead.'

The Colonial Girl *Betty Roberts*

Discussion

1 What happened to Jane? How do you know?

2 What sort of a relationship did Jane have with her mother? Give reasons for your point of view.

3 How does the author of 'The Colonial Girl' prepare her readers for the ending of the story with its leap backwards into the nineteenth century? Give details in your answer and quote from the text.

Activities

1 Imagine that as Jane's mother and father talk about Charles at the party, they notice the young man in naval uniform standing nearby. What do they say about him?

2 Imagine that the storyteller finds his own tombstone in the graveyard. What does it say? (Take your ideas from the story).

3 In your mind, recreate the tale of Charles Fenton, from Essex, England, who was sent as a convict to Tasmania and who worked and died on the property of one of Tasmania's historic country homes, but not before he had been sketched by the daughter of the owner. In a short short story of your own, tell how he died, and why. Try to get some of the flavour of the period into your writing.

Christmas Meeting   *Rosemary Timperley*

Discussion

1 Why did the young man not knock when he came into the woman's room? Explain your answer fully.

2 What sort of a person was Francis Randel? Was he a frightening ghost? Give reasons for your point of view.

3 It is very important to create the right *atmosphere* at the start of a ghost story. Examine the second paragraph of 'Christmas Meeting' which starts: 'It gives me an uncanny feeling …
   a How does Rosemary Timperely build up the atmosphere here?
   b What is the overall mood of the story?

Activities

1 Christmas is not always a time when people celebrate together. In half a page of writing, describe an unusual Christmas scene.

2 Imagine that the old lady never forgot her meeting with Francis Randel. A year later, she was still living in her furnished room. What happened that Christmas Day? Write a page.

3 Write a ghost story of your own. It must include two of the following sentences in it at some point:
   • Her identity remains a mystery.
   • The police checked airports and ferry services.
   • 'I made a mistake, sir,' he said.
   • After all, it was two years.

- 'Bit of a snap decision, my dear?'
- The walk in the dark before midnight ...

The Return   *Marjory E Lambe*

Discussion

1   Whose is the 'low, wicked chuckle by the stairs' at the end of this short short story? What leads you to this conclusion, and what is the significance of it?

2   Why is the title 'The Return' an appropriate one for this story?

3   A *plot* is when one event causes another in a narrative storyline. As EM Forster wrote:
'The king died and then the queen died' is a story. 'The king died, and then the queen died of grief' is a plot.'
Go through the plot of 'The Return' step by step. Here are the first two steps.
  a   Because the old man was a miser, he did not pay his servants properly.
  b   Because he did not pay his servants ...

Activities

1   Write the obituary of the dead servant. You are allowed fifty words (including the headline).

2   Imagine that, as the old man's son wakes up and reaches for his money the morning after the events in 'The Return', he hears a low, wicked chuckle at his bedside. What happens next? Write a page.

3   Write a ghost story of your own. In all ghost stories, a dead person comes back to life in the form of a ghost. Ghosts are no respectors of time, and may reappear after hundreds of years. Not all ghosts are unfriendly or vindictive, but they usually have some 'unfinished business' to attend to before their souls can rest in peace. Here are three suggested starting points.
  - A ghost walks the earth protecting the life of the girl he once loved ...
  - A ghost, killed unjustly, is doomed to re-enact the event every successive year at the same time. There is only one way in which her soul can be laid to rest ...
  - A clumsy ghost has a great deal of trouble controlling his supernatural powers ...

DRAMA

A Deafening
Silence

Vikki Goatham

Vikki Goatham was born in 1962 and raised in Queensland, where she still lives. After studying Journalism, English Literature and Language in the Media at Queensland University, she went on to work as a researcher and freelance journalist before getting married in 1987. She believes that the fiction writer's best tool is personal experience, and her stories now centre around child raising and family life.

Mum's crying in Peter's room again.

It's two whole years since we last saw my older brother Peter. Two whole years since he stormed out of our house angry, half crying with pent-up rage, swearing he would never come back.

And he hasn't.

I will never forget the helpless tears in my mother's eyes as she watched him striding up the road, my father shouting after him, 'Go on, get! If you're so keen to go, go! I don't want to see your ungrateful face in my house again!'

Peter said nothing. He didn't even turn to look back.

The trouble had started weeks, perhaps months before that night. Peter was in his second last year at high school. He didn't want to go on and get his Senior pass but Dad had put the screws on. He did it all in good faith, forcing Peter to continue only because he knew that the unemployment situation was drastic and that the few opportunities available to fifteen-year-old school leavers were mainly menial jobs that would never amount to anything in the future.

Peter detested school. He tried hard in the beginning but his grades were dreadful regardless so he gave up. Nothing bored him more than schoolwork and he often told me how frustrated he felt about it. But I was a year younger and I loved school. How could I help? I didn't even really understand …

Peter knew he had to go on at school. He realized it was the only way to get a worthwhile job but he was also painfully aware that every bad grade he was given decreased his chances of getting one. It was a catch-22 situation.

I remember one evening after he and Dad had had one of their many arguments, Peter went to the bathroom crying — it took a lot to make him cry — and I was dead scared that he would try to kill himself. I know that sounds melodramatic but the razor blades in the bathroom cabinet seemed just too available. I even knocked on the door and made some paltry excuse about thinking I'd left my hairbrush in there just so I could see that he really was all right.

At times our house seemed fit to burst with tension, especially when Peter wanted to go out with mates. Some of his friends had left school and naturally had more personal and monetary freedom than Peter. And worse. Dad always refused when Peter asked if he could go out skating or to the local drive-in theatre with them.

'You don't do your homework, you don't go out!' Dad would say. Every Friday night I slunk into my room and gave myself a pedicure, read a book, anything so that I wasn't on the lounge-room battlefield when Peter asked Dad if he could go out.

Peter was determined to have his way. At first, he asked for Dad's permission every time but after dozens of those inevitable negative replies, he simply *told* Dad he was going, and went. The first night he did this Dad was quite stunned and watched him leave without uttering a word. But the next time he was ready for it and sparks flew. The situation grew progressively worse.

Something I never really understood — still don't understand — is why our mother didn't intervene. She never got involved and let the arguments go on around her. I always felt she had her fingers crossed behind her back, hoping that the whole mess was merely a phase that would eventually pass. But it didn't

Peter and Dad would argue violently time after time. I was always scared they would actually come to blows and Mum would just continue her work in the kitchen as though nothing were wrong. Sometimes I could see the dark shadows about her eyes or the tight thinning of her mouth — those tell-tale signs of strain — but otherwise she gave no indication that she even recognized there was a problem at all. That was, until the night Peter walked out.

He was barely sixteen and he left the house with nothing more than the clothes on his back.

He and Dad had been having their regular argument over homework when Dad exploded as I've never seen him do before or since. I found myself fervently wishing I was not in the room with them, and cringed in the kitchen doorway.

'I'm sick and tired of your lousy attitude, Boy! I've slaved for years to give you a good education and this is the thanks I get. It's not good enough.'

'No! And I'll never be good enough for you, will I?' Peter said bitterly. 'I've always got to be a bit better and do all those things you weren't smart enough to do yourself.'

My father stood up angrily, stubbed out his cigarette butt, and lunged at Peter. Barring the blow with a quick reflex action, Peter protected himself and pushed Dad away.

'Don't Dad! Please …' I couldn't help crying as he came back at Peter using the foulest language I have ever heard him utter. He told Peter that if he felt so strongly about leaving school then he could leave home too.

'I might just do that!' Peter countered.

'You're a useless little no-good!' Dad yelled in much more colourful terms than I dare write.

'And you're a stupid old man!' Peter shouted back.

'I told your mother she should have had an abortion when she was carrying you!' Dad grated out.

There was a crash in the kitchen as Mum dropped a plate.

Peter fell silent.

'That's it!' he hissed after a moment or two, the look in his eyes one of pure hatred. He turned on his heel and went to the kitchen where Mum was tearfully picking up the broken pieces of plate. He knelt down beside her and kissed her cheek. There were tears in his eyes too.

'I can't take it any more Mum,' he said huskily. 'I'm leaving… I love you!'

'I know, son …' I heard Mum whisper back. 'I love you, too!'

I could barely take it in. He meant it. He was going to leave! The determination in his face was unmistakable. He helped Mum put the bits of china into the pedal-bin then walked over to me.

'Bye, sis …' he said in the same low tone as he hugged me. 'Look after yourself. And don't take any of his rot!' he added, glancing quickly at Dad.

'I'll give you rot, Boy! Just you come here!' Dad growled.

'Oh — shut up!' said Peter and he made for the door.

It was like some terrible dream. My mother held me and we both wept as we watched him go. There was nothing we could do.

Dad followed him outside and ranted on until Peter was well out of sight. Then suddenly he was quiet for endless moments before he collapsed on our front lawn and slapped his hands over his face, rocking and weeping like a man tormented.

Unbelievably, my mother took a single deep breath and went resolutely back to the washing up. I followed her.

'Mum! Can't we do *something*?' I wailed. 'He will come back, won't he?'

'Let it be, Kimmy,' she whispered painfully. 'Let it be!'

I ran to my room and must have cried thousands of scalding tears before falling into a restless sleep, clutching my soaked pillow.

I expected Peter to breeze out for breakfast next morning but he did not and our house has never really felt like home since.

Looking back, it seems to me that Peter talked but Dad never listened and Dad yelled so loud that Peter couldn't hear. Now, the silence is deafening.

Mum grieves as though Peter was dead. She doesn't know I've seen her sitting hunched over in his old room crying. She has aged ten years in these two and my father has grown so docile — as though he had all the fight knocked out of him that night.

And for two long years I've waited to hear Peter's voice when I pick up the telephone. I'm certain that one day he *will* call, even if all he says is, 'Hi Mum ... I love you! Bye, sis ... Look after yourself!'

At least it would break this deafening silence ...

Spotlight

Budd Schulberg

Budd Schulberg was born in New York in 1914. He was brought up in Hollywood, and wrote about it in his stories. His satirical novel about the greed of life in Hollywood, *What Makes Sammy Run?*, was published in 1941. He wrote several screenplays, the most famous of which was for *On the Waterfront* which starred Marlon Brando.

The director was trying to bring the picture through in twenty-nine days. The assistant director was trying to impress the director. The second assistant was trying to prove his right to be a first assistant. The three hundred extras were trying to please everybody. The ten-dollar people were trying to fight their way into focus. The seven-and-a-halfs were walking briskly back and forth, doing their perspiring best.

'All right, folks, get *moving*!' the second assistant screamed. 'Now watch me. When I wave this handkerchief, start walking as if you expected to get somewhere.'

'What're ya watching him for?' the first assistant yelled. 'When I drop my hand, start talking it up. You're all happy, see? And make it good! We gotta finish by six sharp.'

The director, running sweat, sleeves rolled up, paced impatiently. 'What's the trouble, boys?' he barked. 'I'm half a day behind now. Get the lead out.'

It was another of those scorching Hollywood afternoons. One of those tough, irritable days. The extras had been at it since nine that morning. When the long-awaited recess came, they crowded around the water cooler.

'After you,' a florid-faced, white-haired old man offered politely. When he was almost trampled in the rush, he took his place philosophically at the end of the line. He mopped his face professionally with an edge of his handkerchief. His calm silence was like a wall of glass cutting him off from the whirlpool of excitement all around him.

Even at the call, 'Take your places, everybody,' he displayed not the slightest trace of emotion. He straightened the dress suit he wore and took his place in the line again.

When the director said, 'Pick me out some people for flash reactions,' excitement stirred the crowd. For some it might mean the chance they had waited and struggled for. For others it meant the extra fifteen dollars they would earn if they were asked to speak a line.

As the old man saw the assistant director descending on him, he waited docilely, like an old horse about to be saddled. But he wasn't sure he wanted this unexpected momentary spotlight. He was old and tired, and this meant strong lights in his eyes and the strain of having to learn new words and speak them within the next few minutes.

But even as he hoped the assistant wasn't going to single him out for a close-up, he was praying that he would. Because extra work had become scarcer and scarcer through the summer; his last job had been two ten-dollar days three weeks ago. That meant pressing the dress suit yourself, and stalling the landlady. Now this additional fifteen dollars would be the difference between keeping the room and packing up again.

Then the assistant was on him. 'All right, Pop, we'll use you.' He stepped into the glare, waiting quietly with eyes half closed as the director opened up on him.

'Okay, old-timer. This'll all be over in a minute — we hope. All you've got to do is smile and say, "I've been waiting here thirty years for this," and he gives you the cue, "On this very spot?" and then you give it this — watch me.' And the director turned his head toward the floor and then quickly looked up again with an unexpected change of expression. 'Get it? Just a different version of that old double take.'

The old man nodded his head slowly. He said he thought he got it.

'Then let's go. See if we can't get it in the can the first time,' the director said, as the juicers hit the lights. He crouched below the cameras, watching the old man critically.

'Hold it. Cut!' he yelled. 'You forgot that double take.'

More nervously, the old man tried again. 'I've been thirty years —'

'For Pete's sake! You forgot "*waiting*"! Waiting — what you're making us do! Take it once more.'

The old man nodded, wetting his lips, trembling. He began again. And again. The director fumed internally. Typical studio economy! Trying to save money with a ten-buck extra instead of paying an actor to do it! The old man fumbled the scene worse each time. He was trying too hard.

'Look, pal. You're making it too tough for yourself. It's just one quick take, see? Just that famous old trick with your eyes and a turn of your head. The thing what's-his-name, Willie Robbins, originated in the old silent days. Think you can do it?'

'I — I think I can do it now,' the old man said.

Everybody hushed again. The cameras started rolling. He made one more tentative stab at it. In vain.

'All right!' the director roared. 'Get back in the crowd — we'll try somebody else.'

And as the old man tried to disappear inconspicuously, he heard the director say, 'For heaven's sake get someone who knows what a double take is!' And an eager, confident extra took his place in the scene.

Back in the crowd of extras, he stood watching his successor. Just in front of him a dumpy elderly woman, one of the visitors to the set, was approaching the handsome young star with her autograph book opened. In a kind of reflex action, the star smiled and reached out for the book. But she had already gone by him! The old man looked up at her in surprise.

'I never thought I'd actually meet you — after all these years,' she said, and she held up the book.

For a moment he stared at her unbelievingly, and then, as he took the book and began to write in it, he seemed to grow broader and taller. He wrote silently, 'As ever, Willie Robbins,' handed the book back with a faint smile, and turned to watch the successful completion of the scene.

The Parasite

Sarah O'Donnell

Sarah O'Donnell was born in Melbourne in 1964. She wrote 'The Parasite' while still a student at Eltham College. Always interested in the complexities of human nature, she studied drama at NIDA, worked with the Elizabethan Theatre Trust, Playbox and MTC, and was Barry Humphries' stage manager on *The Life and Death of Sandy Stone* in 1990. She then went to St Petersberg to study Russian literature.

How it entered her, she didn't know. One day her insides were clean, moving submissively, then suddenly they were contaminated. Some thing began to crawl inside her stomach, living on her, demanding her body as a home. An unclean substance had penetrated, leaving this parasite growing in her belly. Was it something she had eaten, some dirty food? The shame was too great; she was too low to reveal to anyone that inside her body was this monster, too low to ask how she had been infected.

For days her thoughts raced as speedily as the monster grew. Meat left in the sun? Did I not wash it thoroughly enough? Could I possibly have broken the laws of heaven and eaten meat that wasn't kosher? It must have been in some contaminated meat full of blood and hidden evils, not kosher, not clean. Yet it must have been so small, or else I would have seen it. 'Filth, dirt, shame ...' she muttered to herself over and over again.

Then it began to demand. 'Food, give me food,' the parasite told her body. So she filled the cavern beneath her breast. Mother began to ask questions. All that food was making her beautiful daughter fat. Beautiful daughter was becoming ugly with dark-circled eyes and stooping shoulders. The market wasn't big for ugly brides.

The amount of food grew as the parasite did also. It crawled around inside her body exploring areas she never knew existed, each day dominating a little piece more, each day filling the cavern of her insides.

At night the brief respite from the sun would descend and the family would climb to the roof to savour it. Under the middle-eastern sky the heat and dust settled and everything rested, everything, that is, except the parasite. Slithering and pulsating it would not let her be, and down the steps she would have to go once more to satisfy the beast, shuddering as waves of nausea almost brought the food up again.

Each morning when she awoke she hoped it had gone away, but when the stirrings began again, when beneath the masses of flesh she could feel it rising, she would scream inwardly, 'Let go of me!' Then she would go and vomit up the excess food the beast hadn't been able to digest through the night. And the animal sucked and sucked. The beast was sucking out her life's blood; she had never believed that death would take months.

Then it began to show. She could hardly face her family when such guilt was evident. Her mouth never opened, yet her body spoke for itself. In every movement it said, 'Yes I am unclean, more unclean than a leper because I am possessed.'

Her father went about as if nothing were happening, barely noticing his daughter's torture. Mother was concerned; she didn't want her child a fat bride, but as a good wife she waited. One day she gave her husband wine and olives and tentatively approached him. Father plucked a shiny black olive, sucked it and expelled the pip onto mother's clean floor. 'A well-fed daughter is a healthy daughter,' he said, and between generous mouthfuls of wine went on making plans for his daughter's wedding. Mother picked up the pip from the floor; she couldn't stand her domain being dirty.

Gradually and without their help, their daughter was losing control. She didn't speak; she hardly slept; she only satisfied the parasite. More and more alone, she contemplated the duty her parents expected of her. 'Wedding? There will be no wedding. How can there be a wedding when I am falling apart? My father cannot give away a demon with his daughter.' She muttered away; they thought her mad. She ran away.

She had to expel the growth.

The journey was long and tired her. She lay down on the straw and prepared for a death.

The parasite didn't want to leave at first. It put up a fight, holding on with its suckers, refusing to part with her. She contracted her muscles; it pounded in her belly; it tore her as it seeped away.

Through the dim release that she hadn't known for so long a voice disturbed her.

'Mary, Mary, can you hear me? You have a little boy.'

A Deafening Silence   *Vikki Goatham*

Discussion

1 Why did Peter leave home? Give the immediate reason, as well as two other more complex reasons.

2 Was the situation that developed at Peter's home, and which eventually caused Peter to walk out, entirely the fault of Peter's father? Discuss your point of view.

3 Examine the title of this short short story. Does it make any sense? It is an example of an *oxymoron*. Invent some other oxymorons, and explain why you might use them.

Activities

1 **a** In pairs, and in front of the rest of the class, improvise a typical family argument betwen a parent and child. The argument might be about a poor report card, too many parties, or too much watching of television.
   b Next, as a class, discuss how these problems might be overcome with a bit more communication and compromise on both sides.
   c Finally, re-run these scenes incorporating the ideas from the class discussion.

2 Imagine that it is the night of Peter's departure. His mother and father lie in bed, but both are unable to sleep. What do they say to each other? Write a page.

3 Many children run away from home or are forced, for whatever reason, to leave home at an early age. Not all of them end up as drug addicts or child prostitutes. What, for example, do you think happened to Peter? Peter was sensitive, courageous and determined. Write a story about a child who loses the security of family life at an early age. Do not spend time discussing why this happened, but concentrate upon what the child did next. Focus your story on one incident, and take care to describe it in detail.

Spotlight   *Budd Schulberg*

Discussion

1 Why did the director not recognise Willie Robbins? (There are several answers to this question.)

2 This short short story makes us think hard about Hollywood and the nature of fame. What are some of the specific ideas contained in this story? Discuss at least three of them.

3 *Jargon* is the language and vocabulary used by a particular class of society or profession. Often the words and the way they are used are not understood by people from other walks of life.

Pick some examples of film studio jargon from 'Spotlight', and explain how they affect the story and what they add to it.

Activities

1 It is not easy to act out a piece of film or stage business without preparation and practice. Try performing the 'flash reaction' scene that was given to Willie. Do it in front of the rest of the group.

2 a After the day's shooting, the director sits with his two assistants over a beer. They discuss the incident about the white-haired old man. What do they say?

b In groups of three, improvise this scene in front the rest of the group.

3 Whatever happened to so-and-so? We are often surprised to find out, many years later, what happened to our childhood friends. We are also interested to read about famous film stars who end up in the gutter, or popular actors who finish their lives in lonely seclusion. Try writing one of these stories yourself. Here are three suggested approaches.

• Tell a story of an ordinary person, sad or happy, but old, leading an ordinary life. In the last line, name the character. Give him/her a name that we all recognise from our newspapers and magazines today.

• Describe a day in someone's life. During the story, through flashbacks, show what life used to be like for that person. Decide in advance upon the overall effect of your piece: tragic, ironic, moralistic etc.

• A teenager goes to a fortune teller who tells him/her what the future holds in store for him/her. What is the prediction? Does it come true?

The Parasite   *Sarah O'Donnell*

Discussion

1 What is 'The Parasite' about? How do you know?

2 Once you realise what this short short story is about, you are able to compare it to the original story. What aspects of the original story does it illuminate? What details of the original story does it have trouble with, and how does it come to terms with these problems?

3 Look closely at the *vocabulary* of this story. How does the author create a feeling of disgust in the reader by her choice of words?

Activities

1 In pairs, present a 20-minute presentation of this story for another class. First of all, read the story aloud. Next, conduct a discussion session and see what responses are forthcoming.

2 In no more than 200 words, write a review of 'The Parasite' for a local literary magazine.

3 In 'The Parasite', the dramatic moment comes with sudden realisation that this is a story we already know. This is an interesting approach to storytelling, though a difficult one. Try it. First of all choose a subject that is well known to everyone. Give an original slant to the story. Here are three suggestions.
  • The birth of Hitler.*
  • The shooting of President John Kennedy.
  • The Gulf War against Saddam Hussein.

*When you have written your version of this, read Roald Dahl's short short story 'Genesis and Catastrophe'.

Do You Want My Opinion?

ME Kerr

ME Kerr was born in New York. She attended the University of Missouri. She is the author of several books for young adults, including *Am I Trapped Forever?* and *Son of Someone Famous.*

The night before last I dreamed that Cynthia Slater asked my opinion of *The Catcher in the Rye.*

Last night I dreamed I told Lauren Lake what I thought about John Lennon's music, Picasso's art, and Soviet-American relations.

It's getting worse.

I'm tired of putting my head under the cold-water faucet.

Early this morning my father came into my room and said, 'John, are you getting serious with Eleanor Rossi?'

'Just because I took her out three times?'

'Just because you sit up until all hours of the night talking with her!' he said. 'We know all about it, John. Her mother called your mother.'

I didn't say anything. I finished getting on my socks and shoes.

He was standing over me, ready to deliver the lecture. It always started the same way.

'You're going to get in trouble if you're intimate, John. You're too young to let a girl get a hold on you.'

'Nobody has a hold on me, Dad.'

'Not yet. But one thought leads to another. Before you know it, you'll be exploring all sorts of ideas together, knowing each other so well you'll finish each other's sentences.'

'Okay,' I said. 'Okay.'

'Stick to lovemaking.'

'Right,' I said.

'Don't discuss ideas.'

'Dad,' I said, 'kids today — '

'Not nice kids. Aren't you a nice kid?'

'Yeah, I'm a nice kid.'

'And Eleanor, too?'

'Yeah, Eleanor too.'

'Then show some respect for her. Don't ask her opinions. I know it's you who starts it.'

'Okay,' I said.

'Okay?' he said. He mussed up my hair, gave me a poke in the ribs, and went down to breakfast.

By the time I got downstairs, he'd finished his eggs and was sipping coffee, holding hands with my mother.

I don't think they've exchanged an idea in years.

To tell you the truth, I can't imagine them exchanging ideas, ever, though I know they did. She has a collection of letters he wrote to her on every subject from Shakespeare to Bach, and he treasures this little essay she wrote for him when they were engaged, on her feelings about French drama.

All I've ever seen them do is hug and kiss. Maybe they wait until I'm asleep to get into their discussions. Who knows?

I walked to school with Edna O'Leary.

She's very beautiful. I'll say that for her. We put our arms round each other, held tight, and stopped to kiss along the way. But I'd never ask her opinion on any subject. She just doesn't appeal to me that way.

'I love your eyes, John,' she said.

'I love your smile, Edna.'

'Do you like this colour on me?'

'I like you in blue better.'

'Oh, John, that's interesting, because I like you in blue, too.'

We chatted and kissed and laughed as we went up the winding walk to school.

In the schoolyard everyone was cuddled up except for some of the lovers, who were off walking in pairs, talking. I doubted that they were saying trivial things. Their fingers were pointing and their hands were moving, and they were frowning.

You can always tell the ones in love by their passionate gestures as they get into conversations.

I went into the Boys' room for a smoke.

That's right, I'm starting to smoke. That's the state of mind I'm in.

My father says I'm going through a typical teenage stage, but I don't think he understands how crazy it's making me. He says he went through the same thing, but I just can't picture that.

On the bathroom wall there were heads drawn with kids' initials inside.

There was the usual graffiti:

Josephine Merril is a brain! I'd like to know her opinions!

If you'd like some interesting conversation, try Loulou.

I smoked a cigarette and thought of Lauren Lake.

Who didn't think of Lauren? I made a bet with myself that there were half a dozen guys like me remembering Lauren's answer to Mr Porter's question last week in Thoughts class.

A few more answers like that, and those parents who want Thoughts taken out of the school curriculum will have their way. Some kid will run home and tell the folks what goes on in Porter's room, and Thoughts will be replaced by another course in history, language, body maintenance, sex education, or some other boring subject that isn't supposed to be provocative.

'What are dreams?' Mr Porter asked.

Naturally, Lauren's hand shot up first. She can't help herself.

'Lauren?'

'Dreams can be waking thoughts or sleeping thoughts,' she said. 'I had a dream once, a waking one, about a world where you could say anything on your mind, but you had to be very careful about who you touched. You could ask anyone his opinion, but you couldn't just go up and kiss him.'

Some of the kids got red-faced and sucked in their breaths. Even Porter said, 'Now, take it easy, Lauren. Some of your classmates aren't as advanced as you are.'

One kid yelled out, 'If you had to be careful about touching, how would you reproduce in that world?'

'The same way we do in our world,' Lauren said, 'only lovemaking would be a special thing. It would be the intimate thing, and discussing ideas would be a natural thing.'

'That's a good way to cheapen the exchange of ideas!' someone muttered.

Everyone was laughing and nudging the ones next to them, but my mind was spinning. I bet other kids were about to go out of their minds, too.

Mr Porter ran back and kissed Lauren.

She couldn't seem to stop.

She said, 'What's wrong with a free exchange of ideas?'

'Ideas are personal,' someone said. 'Bodies are all alike, but ideas are individual and personal.'

Mr Porter held Lauren's hand. 'Keep it to yourself, Lauren,' he said. 'Just keep it to yourself.'

'In my opinion,' Lauren began, but Mr Porter had to get her under control, so he just pressed his mouth against hers until she was quiet.

'Don't tell *everything* you're thinking, darling,' he warned her. 'I know this is a class on thoughts, but we have to have *some* modesty.'

Lauren just can't quit. She's a brain, and that mind of hers is going to wander all over the place. It just is. She's that kind of girl.

Sometimes I think I'm that kind of boy, and not the nice boy I claim to be. Do you know what I mean? I want to tell someone what I think about the books I read, not just recite the plots. And I want to ask someone what she thinks about World War II, not just go over its history. And I want to …

Never mind.

Listen — the heck with it!

It's not what's up there that counts.

Love makes the world go round. Lovemaking is what's important — relaxing your body, letting your mind empty — just feeling without thinking — just giving in and letting go.

There'll be time enough to exchange ideas, make points — all of it. I'll meet the right girl someday and we'll have the rest of our lives to confide in each other.

'Class come to order!' Mr Porter finally got Lauren quieted down. 'Now, a dream is a succession of images or ideas present in the mind mainly during sleep. It is an involuntary vision …'

On and on, while we all reached for each other's hands, gave each other kisses, and got back to normal.

I put that memory out of my poor messed-up mind, and put out my cigarette.

I was ready to face another day, and I told myself, Hey, you're going to be okay. Tonight, you'll get Dad's car, get a date with someone like Edna O'Leary, go off someplace and whisper loving things into her ear, and feel her soft long blond hair tickle your face, tell her you love her, tell her she's beautiful …

I swung through the door of the Boys' room, and headed down the hall, whistling, walking fast.

Then I saw Lauren, headed right toward me.

She looked carefully at me, and I looked carefully at her.

She frowned a little. I frowned a lot.

I did everything to keep from blurting out, 'Lauren, what do you think about outer space travel?' … 'Lauren, what do you think of Kurt

Vonnegut's writing?' ... 'Lauren, do you think the old Beatles' music is profound or shallow?'

For a moment my mind went blank while we stood without smiling or touching.

Then she kissed my lips, and I slid my arm around her waist.

'Hi, John, dear!' she grinned.

'Hi, Lauren, sweetheart!' I grinned back.

I almost said, 'Would you like to go out tonight?' But it isn't fair to ask a girl out when all you really want is one thing.

I held her very close to me and gently told her that her hair smelled like the sun, and her lips tasted as sweet as red summer apples. Yet all the while I was thinking, Oh, Lauren, we're making a mistake with China, in my opinion ... Oh, Lauren, Lauren, from your point of view, how do things look in the Middle East?

A Snake
Down Under

Glenda Adams

Glenda Adams was born in Sydney in 1940. In 1964 she went to live in New York, where she wrote 'A Snake Down Under' after seeing Nicholas Roeg's Film *Walkabout*. 'I wrote down everything I knew about snakes ... rules ... keeping one's dignity ...' She then pruned her notes, and fashioned her story. Many of her short stories are about her early life, and are often characterised by experimental forms.

We sat in our navy blue serge tunics with white blouses. We sat without moving, our hands on our heads, our feet squarely on the floor under our desks.

The teacher read us a story: A girl got lost in the bush. She wandered all day looking for the way back home. When night fell she took refuge in a cave and fell asleep on the rocky floor. When she awoke she saw to her dismay that a snake had come while she slept and had coiled itself on her warm lap, where it now rested peacefully. The girl did not scream or move lest the snake be aroused and bite her. She stayed still without budging the whole day and the following night, until at last the snake slid away of its own accord. The girl was shocked but unharmed.

We sat on the floor of the gym in our gym uniforms: brown shirts and old-fashioned flared shorts no higher than six inches above the knee, beige ankle socks and brown sneakers. Our mothers had embroidered our initials in gold on the shirt pocket. We sat cross-legged in rows, our backs straight, our hands resting on our knees.

The gym mistress, in ballet slippers, stood before us, her hands clasped before her, her back straight, her stomach muscles firm. She said: If ever a snake should bite you, do not panic. Take a belt or a piece of string and tie a tourniquet around the affected limb between the bite and the heart. Take a sharp knife or razor blade. Make a series of cuts, criss-cross, over the bite. Then, suck at the cuts to remove the poison. Do not swallow. Spit out the blood and the poison. If you have a cut on your gum or lip, get a friend to suck out the poison instead. Then go to the nearest doctor. Try to kill the snake and take it with you. Otherwise, note carefully its distinguishing features.

My friend at school was caught with a copy of *East of Eden*. The headmistress called a special assembly. We stood in rows, at attention, eyes front, half an arm's distance from each other.

The headmistress said: One girl, and I shan't name names, has been reading a book that is highly unsuitable for high school pupils. I shan't name the book, but you know which book I mean. If I find that book inside the school gates again, I will take serious measures. It is hard for some of you to know what is right and what is wrong. Just remember this. If you are thinking of doing something, ask yourself: could I tell my mother about this? If the answer is no, then you can be sure you are doing something wrong.

I know of a girl who went bushwalking and sat on a snake curled up on a rock in the sun. The snake bit her. But since she was with a group that included boys, she was too embarrassed to say anything. So she kept on walking, until the poison overcame her. She fell ill and only then did she admit that a snake had bitten her on a very private part. But it was too late to help her. She died.

When I was sixteen my mother encouraged me to telephone a boy and ask him to be my partner for the school dance. She said: You are old enough to decide who you want to go out with and who you don't want to go out with. I trust you completely.

After that I went out with a Roman Catholic, then an immigrant Dutchman, then an Indonesian.

My mother asked me what I thought I was doing. She said: You can go out with anyone you like as long as it's someone nice.

In the museum were two photographs. In the first, a snake had bitten and killed a young goat. In the second, the snake's jaws were stretched open and the goat was half inside the snake. The outline of the goat's body was visible within the body of the snake. The caption read: Snake trying to eat goat. Once snake begins to eat, it cannot stop. Jaws work like conveyor belt.

A girl on our street suddenly left and went to Queensland for six months. My mother said it was because she had gone too far. She said to me: You know, don't you, that if anything ever happens to you, you can come to me for help. But of course I know you won't ever have to, because you wouldn't ever do anything like that.

Forty minutes of scripture a week was compulsory in all state schools. The Church of England girls sat with hands flat on the desk to preclude fidgeting and note passing. A lay preacher stood before us, his arms upstretched to heaven, his hands and voice shaking. He said: Fornication is a sin and evil. I kissed only one woman, once, before I married. And that was the woman who became my wife. The day I asked her to marry me and she said yes, we sealed our vow with a kiss. I have looked upon no other woman.

I encountered my first snake when I went for an early morning walk beside a wheat field in France. I walked gazing at the sky. When I felt a movement on my leg I looked down. Across my instep rested the tail of a tweedy-skinned snake. The rest of its body was inside the leg of my jeans, resting against my own bare leg. The head was at my knee.

I broke the rules. I screamed and kicked and stamped. The snake fell out of my jeans in a heap and fled into the wheat. I ran back to the house crying.

My friend said, 'Did it offer you an apple?'

The Model

Bernard Malamud

Bernard Malamud was born in 1914 in New York, where he lived for much of his life. After various odd jobs he became a teacher, and it was then that he started writing. He wrote about lonely people, Jews, negroes, examining their role as society's outcasts. In 1967 he won the Pulitzer Prize for his novel *The Fixer*. He died in 1986.

Early one morning, Ephraim Elihu rang up the Art Students League and asked the woman who answered the phone how he could locate an experienced female model he could paint nude. He told the woman that he wanted someone of about thirty. 'Could you possibly help me?'

'I don't recognize your name,' said the woman on the telephone. 'Have you ever dealt with us before? Some of our students will work as models, but usually only for painters we know.' Mr Elihu said he hadn't. He wanted it understood he was an amateur painter who had once studied at the League.

'Do you have a studio?'

'It's a large living room with lots of light. I'm no youngster,' he said, 'but after many years I've begun painting again and I'd like to do some nude studies to get back my feeling for form. I'm not a professional painter, but I'm serious about painting. If you want any references as to my character, I can supply them.'

He asked her what the going rate for models was, and the woman, after a pause, said, 'Six dollars the hour.'

Mr Elihu said that was satisfactory to him. He wanted to talk longer, but she did not encourage him to. She wrote down his name and address and said she thought she could have someone for him the day after tomorrow. He thanked her for her consideration.

That was on Wednesday. The model appeared on Friday morning. She had telephoned the night before, and they had settled on a time for her to come. She rang his bell shortly after nine, and Mr Elihu went at once to the door. He was a gray-haired man of seventy who lived in a brownstone house near Ninth Avenue, and he was excited by the prospect of painting this young woman.

The model was a plain-looking woman of twenty-seven or so, and the painter decided her best features were her eyes. She was wearing a blue raincoat, though it was a clear spring day. The old painter liked her but kept that to himself. She barely glanced at him as she walked firmly into the room.

'Good day,' he said, and she answered, 'Good day.'

'It's like spring,' said the old man. 'The foliage is starting up again.'

'Where do you want me to change?' asked the model.

Mr Elihu asked her her name, and she responded, 'Ms Perry.'

'You can change in the bathroom, I would say, Miss Perry, or if you like, my own room — down the hall — is empty, and you can change there also. It's warmer than the bathroom.'

The model said it made no difference to her but she thought she would rather change in the bathroom.

'That is as you wish,' said the elderly man.

'Is your wife around?' she then asked, glancing into the room.

'No, I happen to be a widower.'

He said he had had a daughter once, but she had died in an accident.

The model said she was sorry. 'I'll change and be out in a few fast minutes.'

'No hurry at all,' said Mr Elihu, glad he was about to paint her.

Ms Perry entered the bathroom, undressed there, and returned quickly. She slipped off her terry-cloth robe. Her head and shoulders were slender and well formed. She asked the old man how he would like her to pose. He was standing by an enamel-top kitchen table near a large window. On the tabletop he had squeezed out, and was mixing together, the contents of two small tubes of paint. There were three other tubes, which he did not touch. The model, taking a last drag of a cigarette, pressed it out against a coffee-can lid on the kitchen table.

'I hope you don't mind if I take a puff once in a while?'

'I don't mind, if you do it when we take a break.'

'That's all I meant.'

She was watching him as he slowly mixed his colors.

Mr Elihu did not immediately look at her nude body but said he would like her to sit in the chair by the window. They were facing a back yard with an ailanthus tree whose leaves had just come out.

'How would you like me to sit, legs crossed or not crossed?'

'However you prefer that. Crossed or uncrossed doesn't make much of a difference to me. Whatever makes you feel comfortable.'

The model seemed surprised at that, but she sat down in the yellow chair by the window and crossed one leg over the other. Her figure was good.

'Is this okay for you?'

Mr Elihu nodded. 'Fine,' he said. 'Very fine.'

He dipped his brush into the paint he had mixed on the tabletop, and after glancing at the model's nude body, began to paint. He would look at her, then look quickly away, as if he were afraid of affronting her. But his expression was objective. He painted apparently casually, from time to time gazing up at the model. He did not often look at her. She seemed not to be aware of him. Once she turned to observe the ailanthus tree, and he studied her momentarily to see what she might have seen in it.

Then she began to watch the painter with interest. She watched his eyes and she watched his hands. He wondered if he was doing something wrong. At the end of about an hour she rose impatiently from the yellow chair.

'Tired?' he asked.

'It isn't that,' she said, 'but I would like to know what in the name of Christ you think you are doing? I frankly don't think you know the first thing about painting.'

She had astonished him. He quickly covered the canvas with a towel.

After a long moment, Mr Elihu, breathing shallowly, wet his dry lips and said he was making no claims for himself as a painter. He said he had tried to make that absolutely clear to the woman he talked to at the art school when he called.

Then he said, 'I might have made a mistake in asking you to come to this house today. I think I should have tested myself a while longer, just so I wouldn't be wasting anybody's time. I guess I am not ready to do what I would like to do.'

'I don't care how long you have tested yourself,' said Ms Perry. 'I honestly don't think you have painted me at all. In fact, I felt you weren't interested in painting me. I think you're interested in letting your eyes go over my naked body for certain reasons of your own. I don't know what your personal needs are, but I'm damn well sure that most of them have nothing to do with painting.'

'I guess I have made a mistake.'

'I guess you have,' said the model. She had her robe on now, the belt pulled tight.

'I'm a painter,' she said, 'and I model because I am broke, but I know a fake when I see one.'

'I wouldn't feel so bad,' said Mr Elihu, 'if I hadn't gone out of my way to explain the situation to that lady at the Art Students League.'

'I'm sorry this happened,' Mr Elihu said hoarsely. 'I should have thought it through more than I did. I'm seventy years of age. I have always loved women and felt a sad loss that I have no particular women friends at this time of my life. That's one of the reasons I wanted to paint again, though I make no claims that I was ever greatly talented. Also, I guess I didn't realize how much about painting I have forgotten. Not only about that, but also about the female body. I didn't realize I would be so moved by yours, and, on reflection, about the way my life has gone. I hoped painting again would refresh my feeling for life. I regret that I have inconvenienced and disturbed you.'

'I'll be paid for my inconvenience,' Ms Perry said, 'but what you can't pay me for is the insult of coming here and submitting myself to your eyes crawling on my body.'

'I didn't mean it as an insult.'

'That's what it feels like to me.'

She then asked Mr Elihu to disrobe.

'I?' he said, surprised. 'What for?'

'I want to sketch you. Take your pants and shirt off.'

He said he had barely got rid of his winter underwear, but she did not smile.

Mr Elihu disrobed, ashamed of how he must look to her.

With quick strokes she sketched his form. He was not a bad-looking man, but felt bad. When she had the sketch, she dipped his brush into a blob of black pigment she had squeezed out of a tube and smeared his features, leaving a black mess.

He watched her hating him, but said nothing.

Ms Perry tossed the brush into a wastebasket and returned to the bathroom for her clothing.

The old man wrote out a check for her for the sum they had agreed on. He was ashamed to sign his name, but he signed it and handed it to her. Ms Perry slipped the check into her large purse and left.

He thought that in her way she was not a bad-looking woman, though she lacked grace. The old man then asked himself, 'Is there nothing more to my life than it is now? Is this all that is left to me?'

The answer seemed to be yes, and he wept at how old he had so quickly become.

Afterward he removed the towel over his canvas and tried to fill in her face, but he had already forgotten it.

Do You Want My Opinion? *ME Kerr*

Discussion

1   At what point in the story did you become aware of what exactly was going on? Locate the line. Give your reasons.

2   What are some of the ideas the author is asking us to consider in 'Do You Want My Opinion'? Discuss at least three of them.

3   An *allusion* is a passing reference to something. If a writer alludes to something she/he refers to it but does not explain it. You are expected to know what the writer is talking about. Find all the allusions in this short short story, and explain them.

Activities

1   Write the first page of a 'dirty book' published in John's world.

2   It is the evening after the 'dreams' lesson in Mr Porter's Thoughts class. What would Laura Lake, Mr Porter and another student from the class think of the incident? Record their responses in a paragraph for each person.

3   Write a story of your own in which social attitudes and values have been turned around. If you have trouble finding ideas, here are three suggestions. You might like to write about a world in which:
   *   athletes are social outcasts
   *   those who do not rise in the ranks are considered successful
   *   big is beautiful.

A Snake Down Under   *Glenda Adams*

Discussion

1   In one sentence, say what 'A Snake Down Under' is about.

2   What are some of the ideas the author is asking us to consider in this short short story? Discuss at least three of them.

3   'A Snake Down Under' is an example of *episodic writing*. Each section is complete in itself; there is no continuity from one section to the next. What are some of the effects of this style of writing?

Activities

1 Photocopy this story. Cut it up into its nine separate sections. Experiment by rearranging these sections into different orders, and see what changes are made to the original piece in each case. What have you discovered?

2 'If you are thinking of doing something, ask yourself: could I tell my mother about this? If the answer is no, then you can be sure you are doing something wrong.'

   Do you agree with this? Discuss your thoughts on this matter, giving specific examples, in a page of writing.

3 'A Snake Down Under' is told in nine short scenes. Each scene is static (i.e. each scene presents an isolated picture or episode). No scene runs diretly into another. Yet each scene is like a facet of a diamond, for all the scenes are needed to make up the whole. Try writing in this way yourself. Choose your topic carefully, for example, take an abstract idea — write about beauty, responsibility, luck or ambition.

The Model *Bernard Malamud*

Discussion

1 Was the old man a sex maniac? Give reasons for your point of view.

2 What went wrong, exactly, in the episode between Ephraim Elihu and the model?

3 The *setting* of a story is important. First, the description of the location helps to establish the background for the rest of the story. Second, the setting can become a key to the personality and attitude of the characters. Discuss the importance of the setting in 'The Model': Ephraim Elihu's private house, springtime.

Activities

1 Imagine that Ephraim Elihu has advertised for a model in his local newspaper. He has paid for twenty words exactly. Using your knowledge of how Ephraim Elihu chooses and uses words, write his advertisement for him.

2 Imagine that the model lives with her mother. What happens when she gets home that evening after her session with Ephraim Elihu, and what do the two women say to each other?

3 Much of the poignancy of this story comes about because of a meeting between a young girl and an older man who do not understand each other. Try turning this around. Write a story of your own in which a young man is thrown into the company of an older woman. Build your story around one incident only. Choose your setting carefully. Here are three suggestions.
  • The man comes to repair the woman's washing machine.
  • One is blind, the other a voluntary community services helper.
  • He is an ambitious young businessman who discovers that his new boss is a woman.

Examination Day

Henry Slesar

Henry Slesar is an American short story writer who specialises in stories of horror, suspense and the macabre. 'Examination Day' seems ordinary enough at the start, but it shocks us with its unexpected twist, and ends by making us think hard about our social values.

The Jordans never spoke of the exam, not until their son, Dickie, was twelve years old. It was on his birthday that Mrs Jordan first mentioned the subject in his presence, and the anxious manner of her speech caused her husband to answer sharply.

'Forget about it,' he said. 'He'll do all right.'

They were at the breakfast table, and the boy looked up from his plate curiously. He was an alert-eyed youngster, with flat blond hair and a quick, nervous manner. He didn't understand what the sudden tension was about, but he did know that today was his birthday, and he wanted harmony above all. Somewhere in the little apartment there were wrapped, beribboned packages waiting to be opened, and in the tiny wall-kitchen something warm and sweet was being prepared in the automatic stove. He wanted the day to be happy, and the moistness of his mother's eyes, the scowl on his father's face, spoiled the mood of fluttering expectation with which he had greeted the morning.

'What exam?' he asked.

His mother looked at the tablecloth. 'It's just a sort of Government intelligence test they give children at the age of twelve. You'll be taking it next week. It's nothing to worry about.'

'You mean a test like in school?'

'Something like that,' his father said, getting up from the table. 'Go and read your comics, Dickie.' The boy rose and wandered towards that part of the living room which had been 'his' corner since infancy. He fingered the topmost comic of the stack, but seemed uninterested in the colourful squares of fast-paced action. He wandered towards the window, and peered gloomily at the veil of mist that shrouded the glass.

'Why did it have to rain today?' he said. 'Why couldn't it rain tomorrow?'

His father, now slumped into an armchair with the Government newspaper, rattled the sheets in vexation. 'Because it just did, that's all. Rain makes the grass grow.'

'Why, Dad?'

'Because it does, that's all.'

Dickie puckered his brow. 'What makes it green, though? The grass?'

'Nobody knows,' his father snapped, then immediately regretted his abruptness.

Later in the day, it was birthday time again. His mother beamed as she handed over the gaily coloured packages, and even his father managed a grin and a rumple-of-the-hair. He kissed his mother and shook hands gravely with his father. Then the birthday cake was brought forth, and the ceremonies concluded.

An hour later, seated by the window, he watched the sun force its way between the clouds.

'Dad,' he said, 'how far away is the sun?'

'Five thousand miles,' his father said.

Dickie sat at the breakfast table and again saw moisture in his mother's eyes. He didn't connect her tears with the exam until his father suddenly brought the subject to light again.

'Well, Dickie,' he said, with a manly frown, 'you've got an appointment today.'

'I know Dad. I hope —'

'Now, it's nothing to worry about. Thousands of children take this test every day. The Government wants to know how smart you are, Dickie. That's all there is to it.'

'I get good marks in school,' he said hesitantly.

'This is different. This is a — special kind of test. They give you this stuff to drink, you see, and then you go into a room where there's a sort of machine —'

'What stuff to drink?' Dickie said.

'It's nothing. It tastes like peppermint. It's just to make sure you answer the questions truthfully. Not that the Government thinks you won't tell the truth, but this stuff makes sure.'

Dickie's face showed puzzlement, and a touch of fright. He looked at his mother, and she composed her face into a misty smile.

'Everything will be all right,' she said.

'Of course it will,' his father agreed. 'You're a good boy, Dickie; you'll make out fine. Then we'll come home and celebrate. All right?'

'Yes, sir,' Dickie said.

They entered the Government Educational Building fifteen minutes before the appointed hour. They crossed the marble floors of the great pillared lobby, passed beneath an archway and entered an automatic lift that brought them to the fourth floor.

There was a young man wearing an insignia-less tunic, seated at a polished desk in front of Room 404. He held a clipboard in his hand, and he checked the list down to the Js and permitted the Jordans to enter.

The room was as cold and official as a courtroom, with long benches flanking metal tables. There were several fathers and sons already there, and a thin-lipped woman with cropped black hair was passing out sheets of paper.

Mr Jordan filled out the form, and returned it to the clerk. Then he told Dickie: 'It won't be long now. When they call your name, you just go through the doorway at that end of the room.' He indicated the portal with his finger.

A concealed loudspeaker crackled and called off the first name. Dickie saw a boy leave his father's side reluctantly and walk slowly towards the door.

At five minutes to eleven, they called the name of Jordan.

'Good luck, son,' his father said, without looking at him. 'I'll call for you when the test is over.'

Dickie walked to the door and turned the knob. The room inside was dim, and he could barely make out the features of the grey-tunicked attendant who greeted him.

'Sit down,' the man said softly. He indicated a high stool beside his desk. 'Your name's Richard Jordan?'

'Yes, sir.'

'Your classification number is 600–115. Drink this, Richard.'

He lifted a plastic cup from the desk and handed it to the boy. The liquid inside had the consistency of buttermilk, tasted only vaguely of the promised peppermint. Dickie downed it, and handed the man the empty cup.

He sat in silence, feeling drowsy, while the man wrote busily on a sheet of paper. Then the attendant looked at his watch, and rose to stand only inches from Dickie's face. He unclipped a penlike object from the pocket of his tunic, and flashed a tiny light into the boy's eyes.

'All right,' he said. 'Come with me, Richard.'

He led Dickie to the end of the room, where a single wooden arm-chair faced a multi-dialled computing machine. There was a microphone on the left arm of the chair, and when the boy sat down, he found its pinpoint head conveniently at his mouth.

'Now just relax, Richard. You'll be asked some questions, and you think them over carefully. Then give your answers into the microphone. The machine will take care of the rest.'

'Yes, sir.'

'I'll leave you alone now. Whenever you want to start, just say "ready" into the microphone.'

'Yes, sir.'

The man squeezed his shoulder, and left.

Dickie said, 'Ready.'

Lights appeared on the machine, and a mechanism whirred. A voice said:

'Complete this sequence. One, four, seven, ten ...'

Mr and Mrs Jordan were in the living room, not speaking, not even speculating.

It was almost four o'clock when the telephone rang. The woman tried to reach it first, but her husband was quicker.

'Mr Jordan?'

The voice was clipped; a brisk, official voice.

'Yes, speaking.'

'This is the Government Educational Service. Your son, Richard M. Jordan, Classification 600–115, has completed the Government examination. We regret to inform you that his intelligence quotient is above the Government regulation, according to Rule 84, Section 5, of the New Code.'

Across the room, the woman cried out, knowing nothing except the emotion she read on her husband's face.

'You may specify by telephone,' the voice droned on, 'whether you wish his body interred by the Government, or would you prefer a private burial place? The fee for Government burial is ten dollars.'

The Wife's
Story

Ursula Le Guin

Ursula Le Guin was born in California in 1929. She is best known for her fantasy and science fiction writing. Her imagination has given these genres new and innovative dimensions. She has broadened them to include a female perspective that was lacking before. *A Wizard of Earthsea* is one of the classics of twentieth-century fantasy, while *The Left Hand of Darkness* and *The Dispossessed* have each won the Hugo and Nebula Awards.

He was a good husband, a good father. I don't understand it. I don't believe in it. I don't believe that it happened. I saw it happen but it isn't true. It can't be. He was always gentle. If you'd have seen him playing with the children, anybody who saw him with the children would have known that there wasn't any bad in him, not one mean bone. When I first met him he was still living with his mother, over near Spring Lake, and I used to see them together, the mother and the sons, and think that any young fellow that was that nice with his family must be one worth knowing. Then one time when I was walking in the woods I met him by himself coming back from a hunting trip. He hadn't got any game at all, not so much as a field mouse, but he wasn't cast down about it. He was just larking along enjoying the morning air. That's one of the things I first loved about him. He didn't take things hard, he didn't grouch and whine when things didn't go his way. So we got to talking that day. And I guess things moved right along after that, because pretty soon he was over here pretty near all the time. And my sister said — see, my parents had moved out the year before and gone south, leaving us the place — my sister said, kind of teasing but serious, 'Well! If he's going to be here every day and half the night, I guess there isn't room for me!' And she moved out — just down the way. We've always been real close, her and me. That's the sort of thing doesn't ever change. I couldn't ever have got through this bad time without my sis.

Well, so he come to live here. And all I can say is, it was the happy year of my life. He was just purely good to me. A hard worker and never lazy, and so big and fine-looking. Everybody looked up to him, you know, young as he was. Lodge Meeting nights, more and more often they had him to lead the singing. He had such a beautiful voice, and he'd lead off strong, and the others following and joining in, high voices and low. It brings the shivers on me now to think of it, hearing it, nights when I'd stayed home from meeting when the children was babies — the singing coming up through the trees there, and the moonlight, summer nights, the full moon shining. I'll never hear anything so beautiful. I'll never know a joy like that again.

It was the moon, that's what they say. It's the moon's fault, and the blood. It was in his father's blood. I never knew his father, and now I wonder what become of him. He was from up Whitewater way, and had no kin around here. I always thought he went back there, but now I don't know. There was some talk about him, tales that come out after what happened to my husband. It's something runs in the blood, they say, and it may never come out, but if it does, it's the change of the moon that does it. Always it happens in the dark of the moon. When everybody's home and asleep. Something comes over the one that's got the curse in his blood, they say, and he gets up because he can't sleep and goes out into the glaring sun, and goes off all alone — drawn to find those like him.

And it may be so, because my husband would do that. I'd half rouse and say, 'Where are you going to?' and he'd say, 'Oh, hunting, be back this evening,' and it wasn't like him, even his voice was different. But I'd be so sleepy, and not wanting to wake the kids, and he was so good and responsible, it was no call of mine to go asking, 'Why?' and 'Where?' and all like that.

So it happened that way maybe three times or four. He'd come back late, and worn out, and pretty near cross for one so sweet tempered — not wanting to talk about it. I figured everybody got to bust out now and then, and nagging never helped anything. But it did begin to worry me. Not so much that he went, but that he come back so tired and strange. Even, he smelled strange. It made my hair stand up on end. I could not endure it and I said, 'What is that — those smells on you? All over you!' And he said, 'I don't know,' real short, and made like he was sleeping. But he went down when he thought I wasn't noticing, and washed and washed himself. But those smells stayed in his hair, and in our bed, for days.

And then the awful thing. I don't find it easy to tell about this. I want to cry when I have to bring it to my mind. Our youngest, the little one, my baby, she turned from her father, just overnight. He come in and she got scared-looking, stiff, with her eyes wide, and then she began to cry and try to hide behind me. She didn't yet talk plain but she was saying over and over, 'Make it go away! Make it go away!'

The look in his eyes, just for one moment, when he heard that. That's what I don't want ever to remember. That's what I can't forget. The look in his eyes looking at his own child.

I said to the child, 'Shame on you, what's got into you!' — scolding, but keeping her right up close to me at the same time, because I was frightened too. Frightened to shaking.

He looked away then and said something like, 'Guess she just waked up dreaming,' and passed it off that way. Or tried to. And so did I. And I got real mad with my baby when she kept on acting crazy scared of her own dad. But she couldn't help it and I couldn't change it.

He kept away that whole day. Because he knew, I guess. It was just beginning dark of the moon.

It was hot and close inside, and dark, and we'd all been asleep some while, when something woke me up. He wasn't there beside me. I heard a little stir in the passage, when I listened. So I got up, because I could bear it no longer. I went out into the passage, and it was light there, hard sun-light coming in from the door. And I saw him standing just outside, in the tall grass by the entrance. His head was hanging. Presently he sat down, like he felt weary, and looked down at his feet. I held still, inside and watched — I don't know what for.

And I saw what he saw. I saw the changing. In his feet, it was, first. They got long, each foot got longer, stretching out, the toes stretching out and the foot getting long, and fleshy, and white. And no hair on them.

The hair begun to come away all over his body. It was like his hair fried away in the sunlight and was gone. He was white all over, then, like a worm's skin. And he turned his face. It was changing while I looked. *It got flatter and flatter, the mouth flat and wide*, and the teeth grinning flat and dull, and the nose just a knob of flesh with nostril holes, and the ears gone, and the eyes gone blue — blue, with white rims around the blue — staring at me out of that flat, soft, white face.

He stood up then on two legs.

I saw him, I had to see him, my own dear love, turned into the hate-ful one.

I couldn't move, but as I crouched there in the passage staring out into the day I was trembling and shaking with a growl that burst out into a crazy, awful howling. A grief howl and a terror howl and a calling howl. And the others heard it, even sleeping, and woke up.

It stared and peered, that thing my husband had turned into, and shoved its face up to the entrance of our house. I was still bound by mortal fear, but behind me the children had waked up, and the baby was whimpering. The mother anger come into me then, and I snarled and crept forward.

The man thing looked around. It had no gun, like the ones from the man places do. But it picked up a heavy fallen tree branch in its long white foot, and shoved the end of that down into our house, at me. I snapped the end of it in my teeth and started to force my way out, because I knew the man would kill our children if it could. But my sister was already coming. I saw her running at the man with her head low and her mane high and her eyes yellow as the winter sun. It turned on her and raised up that branch to hit her. But I come out of the doorway, mad with the mother anger, and the others all were coming answering my call, the whole pack gathering, there in that blind glare and heat of the sun at noon.

The man looked round at us and yelled out loud, and brandished the branch it held. Then it broke and ran, heading for the cleared fields and plowlands, down the mountainside. It ran, on two legs, leaping and weaving, and we followed it.

I was last, because love still bound the anger and the fear in me. I was running when I saw them pull it down. My sister's teeth were in its throat. I got there and it was dead. The others were drawing back from the kill, because of the taste of the blood, and the smell. The younger ones were cowering and some crying, and my sister rubbed her mouth against her forelegs over and over to get rid of the taste. I went up close because I thought if the thing was dead the spell, the curse must be done, and my husband would come back — alive, or even dead, if I could only see him, my true love, in his true form, beautiful. But only the dead man lay there white and bloody. We drew back and back from it, and turned and ran, back up into the hills, back to the woods of the shadows and the twilight and the blessed dark.

The Falling Girl

Dino Buzzati

Translated by Lawrence Venuti from the Italian

Dino Buzzati was born in 1906 in Milan. For most of his life, he worked as a journalist, covering politics and science, but also more unusual phenomena such as UFO sightings and exorcisms. He had a strong sense of the absurd, and enjoyed writing about dreams, sci-fi tales and fantasies.

Marta was nineteen. She looked out over the roof of the skyscraper, and seeing the city below shining in the dusk, she was overcome with dizziness.

The skyscraper was silver, supreme and fortunate in that most beautiful and pure evening, as here and there the wind stirred a few fine filaments of cloud against an absolutely incredible blue background. It was in fact the hour when the city is seized by inspiration and whoever is not blind is swept away by it. From that airy height the girl saw the streets and the masses of buildings writhing in the long spasm of sunset, and at the point where the white of the houses ended, the blue of the sea began. Seen from above, the sea looked as if it were rising. And since the veils of the night were advancing from the east, the city became a sweet abyss burning with pulsating lights. Within it were powerful men, and women who were even more powerful, furs and violins, cars glossy as onyx, the neon signs of nightclubs, the entrance halls of darkened mansions, fountains, diamonds, old silent gardens, parties, desires, affairs, and, above all, that consuming sorcery of the evening which provokes dreams of greatness and glory.

Seeing these things, Marta hopelessly leaned out over the railing and let herself go. She felt as if she were hovering in the air, but she was falling. Given the extraordinary height of the skyscraper, the streets and squares down at the bottom were very far away. Who knows how long it would take her to get there. Yet the girl was falling.

At that hour the terraces and balconies of the top floors were filled with rich and elegant people who were having cocktails and making silly conversation. They were scattered in crowds, and their talk muffled the music. Marta passed before them and several people looked out to watch her.

Flights of that kind (mostly by girls, in fact) were not rare in the sky-scraper and they constituted an interesting diversion for the tenants; this was also the reason why the price of those apartments was very high.

The sun had not yet completely set and it did its best to illuminate Marta's simple clothing. She wore a modest, inexpensive spring dress bought off the rack. Yet the lyrical light of the sunset exalted it some-what, making it chic.

From the millionaires' balconies, gallant hands were stretched out toward her, offering flowers and cocktails. 'Miss, would you like a drink? … Gentle butterfly, why not stop a minute with us?'

She laughed, hovering, happy (but meanwhile she was falling): 'No, thanks, friends. I can't. I'm in a hurry.'

'Where are you headed?' they asked her.

'Ah, don't make me say,' Marta answered, waving her hands in a friendly good-bye.

A young man, tall, dark, very distinguished, extended an arm to snatch her. She liked him. And yet Marta quickly defended herself: 'How dare you, sir?' and she had time to give him a little tap on the nose.

The beautiful people, then, were interested in her and that filled her with satisfaction. She felt fascinating, stylish. On the flower-filled ter-races, amid the bustle of waiters in white and the bursts of exotic songs, there was talk for a few minutes, perhaps less, of the young woman who was passing by (from top to bottom, on a vertical course). Some thought her pretty, others thought her so-so, everyone found her interesting.

'You have your entire life before you,' they told her, 'why are you in such a hurry? You still have time to rush around and busy yourself. Stop with us for a little while, it's only a modest little party among friends, really, you'll have a good time.'

She made an attempt to answer but the force of gravity had already quickly carried her to the floor below, then two, three, four floors below; in fact, exactly as you gaily rush around when you are just nineteen years old.

Of course, the distance that separated her from the bottom, that is, from street level, was immense. It is true that she began falling just a little while ago, but the street always seemed very far away.

In the meantime, however, the sun had plunged into the sea; one could see it disappear, transformed into a shimmering reddish mushroom. As a result, it no longer emitted its vivifying rays to light up the girl's dress and make her a seductive comet. It was a good thing that the windows and terraces of the skyscraper were almost all illuminated and the bright reflections completely gilded her as she gradually passed by.

Now Marta no longer saw just groups of carefree people inside the apartments; at times there were even some businesses where the employees, in black or blue aprons, were sitting at desks in long rows. Several of them were young people as old as or older than she, and weary of the day by now, every once in a while they raised their eyes from their duties and from typewriters. In this way they too saw her, and a few ran to the windows. 'Where are you going? Why so fast? Who are you?' they shouted to her. One could divine something akin to envy in their words.

'They're waiting for me down there,' she answered. 'I can't stop. Forgive me.' And again she laughed, wavering on her headlong fall, but it wasn't like her previous laughter anymore. The night had craftily fallen and Marta started to feel cold.

Meanwhile, looking downward, she saw a bright halo of lights at the entrance of a building. Here long black cars were stopping (from the great distance they looked as small as ants), and men and women were getting out, anxious to go inside. She seemed to make out the sparkling of jewels in that swarm. Above the entrance flags were flying.

They were obviously giving a large party, exactly the kind that Marta dreamed of ever since she was a child. Heaven help her if she missed it. Down there opportunity was waiting for her, fate, romance, the true inauguration of her life. Would she arrive in time?

She spitefully noticed that another girl was falling about thirty meters above her. She was decidedly prettier than Marta and she wore a rather classy evening gown. For some unknown reason she came down much faster than Marta, so that in a few moments she passed by her and disappeared below, even though Marta was calling her. Without doubt she would get to the party before Marta; perhaps she had a plan all worked out to supplant her.

Then she realized that they weren't alone. Along the sides of the skyscraper many other young women were plunging downward, their faces taut with the excitement of the flight, their hands cheerfully waving as if to say: look at us, here we are, entertain us, is not the world ours?

It was a contest, then. And she only had a shabby little dress while those other girls were dressed smartly like high-fashion models and some even wrapped luxurious mink stoles tightly around their bare shoulders. So self-assured when she began the leap, Marta now felt a tremor growing inside her; perhaps it was just the cold; but it may have been fear too, the fear of having made an error without remedy.

It seemed to be late at night now. The windows were darkened one after another, the echoes of music became more rare, the offices were empty, young men no longer leaned out from the windowsills extending their hands. What time was it? At the entrance to the building down below — which in the meantime had grown larger, and one could now distinguish all the architectural details — the lights were still burning, but the bustle of cars had stopped. Every now and then, in fact, small groups of people came out of the main floor wearily drawing away. Then the lights of the entrance were also turned off.

Marta felt her heart tightening. Alas, she wouldn't reach the ball in time. Glancing upwards, she saw the pinnacle of the skyscraper in all its cruel power. It was almost completely dark. On the top floors a few windows here and there were still lit. And above the top the first glimmer of dawn was spreading.

In a dining recess on the twenty-eighth floor a man about forty years old was having his morning coffee and reading his newspaper while his wife tidied up the room. A clock on the sideboard indicated 8:45. A shadow suddenly passed before the window .

'Alberto!' the wife shouted. 'Did you see that? A woman passed by.'

'Who was it?' he said without raising his eyes from the newspaper.

'An old woman,' the wife answered. 'A decrepit old woman. She looked frightened.'

'It's always like that,' the man muttered. 'At these low floors only falling old women pass by. You can see beautiful girls from the hundred-and-fiftieth floor up. Those apartments don't cost so much for nothing.'

'At least down here there's the advantage,' observed the wife, 'that you can hear the thud when they touch the ground.'

'This time not even that,' he said, shaking his head, after he stood listening for a few minutes. Then he had another sip of coffee.

Examination Day   *Henry Slesar*

Discussion

1   Analyse why Dickie's father told him that the sun was five thousand miles away.

2   Although fantastic, stories of this kind often give us a clear insight into some aspect of our own civilisation. What do you think Henry Slesar might be asking his readers to think about in this short short story?

3   A *cliché* is a sentence or phrase that has been used so frequently that it has become empty of meaning. What do clichés tell us about those who use them in their own speech? Examine the clichés in 'Examination Day' in this light. (This story contains perhaps the most often-used cliché from TV soap and drama dialogue. Can you pick it?)

Activities

1   Richard's test is over. Two officials from the Government Educational Service are talking, prior to ringing up Richard's parents with the results. In a page, record their conversation.

2   At what point in the story did you realise that Dickie Jordan's world was not our world? What sort of a world do you think it might be, where a Government passes New Codes of the sort referred to in 'Examination Day'? Write a page.

3   Write a story about Richard's younger brother, Brad Jordan, who enjoyed reading his comics when young and never asked awkward questions of his parents. What has happened to him now? Describe Brad's world and work when he is either 20, 40 or 60 years old. Take any clues you like from Slesar's original story.

The Wife's Story   *Ursula Le Guin*

Discussion

1   At what point in the story did you become aware of what was happening? Locate the line. Give your reasons.

2   By showing the human form as being so ugly, what is the author of 'The Wife's Story' asking her readers to experience? Does she wish to make us consider any specific ideas, do you think, and, if so, what?

3 Examine the *lengths of sentences* used in this short short story. To start with, there are several short sentences. What is the effect of this? At other points, a long sentence is followed by a short one. (Read from: 'It got flatter and flatter, the mouth flat and wide …') What is the effect of this? Are there any other observations you can make about sentence length in this story?

Activities

1 Write the first ten lines of a fantasy story entitled 'The Husband's Story'.

2 In Le Guin's story, a human being is described through the eyes of a wolf. Imagine that the same wolf pack arrives on the outskirts of a town. What do the wolves see? How do they interepret what they see? Describe an everyday incident, showing human behaviour through the eyes of wild animals.

3 Fantasy stories are all highly original pieces, the products of inventive minds and fertile imaginations. There is no formula for writing these stories. The best ones give us an insight into our own natures, or force us to question or reconsider the values we live with or what we have always thought of as being the basic 'truths' of our existence.
    In fantasy, anything can happen. Try writing a fantasy story. Here are three ideas to get you thinking.
- A man deliberately gives himself up to be eaten alive by a beautiful but dangerous flower.
- A girl from the twenty-second century suddenly finds herself in present-day Sydney.
- Life becomes a frightening large-scale version of a popular television quiz game.

The Falling Girl   *Dino Buzzati*

Discussion

1 How does the story end? Does Marta ever land after falling from the skyscraper?

2 What is 'The Falling Girl' about, do you think? What are some of the ideas the author is presenting to us in this short short story? Discuss at least three of them.

3 An *image* is a 'word picture' projected onto the back of the mind. Look at the imagery in 'The Falling Girl'. What sort of imagery does Dino Buzzati use in this story? How important is the imagery to the story, and why?

Activities

1 The description of the city from the skyscraper (paragraph two) establishes the atmosphere for the rest of the story. Without looking back at it, describe this city scene in your own words. Compare your description with Buzzati's. What words does he use that you do not?

2 Taking your inspiration from Buzzati, describe a nightmare of your own, keeping as close to his style of writing as possible.

3 There is an allegorical quality to this story. Marta's fall, although fantastic, is her journey through life. How do you see life? As a fall, perhaps, or a rowing boat race, or a game of blind man's buff. Some see it as a jail sentence; others as a cricket match. Find your own allegorical imagery and write a tale of fantasy around it. How will it end?

The Chaser

John Collier

John Collier was born in England, though he has spent most of his life in
America. His stories border on the macabre, ranging from horror to fantasy.
They often have an original and unexpected twist to them, and are
characterised by sharp and cynical insights into the human condition.

Alan Austen, as nervous as a kitten, went up certain dark and creaky
stairs in the neighbourhood of Pell Street, and peered about for a long
time on the dim landing before he found the name he wanted written
obscurely on one of the doors.

He pushed open this door, as he had been told to do, and found
himself in a tiny room, which contained no furniture but a plain kitchen
table, a rocking chair, and an ordinary chair. On one of the dirty buff-
coloured walls were a couple of shelves, containing in all perhaps a dozen
bottles and jars.

An old man sat in the rocking chair, reading a newspaper. Alan, without a word, handed him the card he had been given. 'Sit down, Mr
Austen,' said the old man very politely. 'I am glad to make your acquain-
tance.'

'Is it true,' asked Alan, 'that you have a certain mixture that has — er
— quite extraordinary effects?'

'My dear sir,' replied the old man, 'my stock in trade is not very large
— I don't deal in laxatives and teething mixtures — but, such as it is, it is
varied. I think nothing I sell has effects which could be precisely
described as ordinary.'

'Well the fact is —' began Alan.

'Here, for example,' interrupted the old man, reaching for a bottle
from the shelf. 'Here is a liquid as colourless as water, almost tasteless,

quite imperceptible in coffee, milk, wine, or any other beverage. It is also quite imperceptible to any known method of autopsy.'

'Do you mean it is a poison?' cried Alan, very much horrified.

'Call it cleaning fluid if you like,' said the old man indifferently. 'Lives need cleaning. Call it a spot-remover. "Out, damned spot!" Eh? "Out, brief candle!"'

'I want nothing of that sort,' said Alan.

'Probably it is just as well,' said the old man. 'Do you know the price of this? For one teaspoonful, which is sufficient, I ask five thousand dollars. Never less. Not a penny less.'

'I hope all your mixtures are not as expensive,' said Alan apprehensively.

'Oh, dear, no,' said the old man. 'It would be no good charging that sort of price for a love-potion, for example. Young people who need a love potion very seldom have five thousand dollars. If they had they would not need a love potion.'

'I'm glad to hear you say so,' said Alan.

'I look at it like this,' said the old man. 'Please a customer with one article, and he will come back when he needs another. Even if it is more costly. He will save up for it, if necessary.'

'So,' said Alan, 'you really do sell love potions?'

'If I did not sell love-potions,' said the old man, reaching for another bottle, 'I should not have mentioned the other matter to you. It is only when one is in a position to oblige that one can afford to be so confidential.'

'And these potions,' said Alan. 'They are not just — just — er —'

'Oh, no.' said the old man. 'Their effects are permanent, and extend far beyond the mere carnal impulse. But they include it. Oh, yes, they include it. Bountifully. Insistently. Everlastingly.'

'Dear me!' said Alan, attempting a look of scientific detachment. 'How very interesting!'

'But consider the spiritual side,' said the old man.

'I do, indeed,' said Alan.

'For indifference,' said the old man, 'they substitute devotion. For scorn, adoration. Give one tiny measure of this to the young lady — its flavour is imperceptible in orange juice, soup or cocktails — and however gay and giddy she is, she will change altogether. She'll want nothing but solitude, and you.'

'I can hardly believe it,' said Alan. 'She is so fond of parties.'

'She will not like them anymore,' said the old man. 'She'll be afraid of the pretty girls you may meet.'

'She'll actually be jealous?' cried Alan in a rapture. 'Of me?'

'Yes, she will want to be everything to you.'

'She is, already. Only she doesn't care about it.'

'She will, when she has taken this. She will care immensely. You'll be her sole interest in life.'

'Wonderful!' cried Alan.

'She'll want to know all you do,' said the old man. 'All that has happened to you during the day. Every word of it. She'll want to know what you are thinking about, why you smile suddenly, why you are looking sad.'

'That is love!' cried Alan.

'Yes,' said the old man. 'How carefully she'll look after you! She'll never allow you to be tired, to sit in a draught, to neglect your food. If you are an hour late, she'll be terrified. She'll think you are killed, or that some siren has caught you.'

'I can hardly imagine Diana like that!' cried Alan, overwhelmed with joy.

'You will not have to use your imagination,' said the old man. 'And, by the way, since there are always sirens, if by any chance you *should*, later on, slip a little, you need not worry. She will forgive you, in the end. She'll be terribly hurt, of course, but she'll forgive you — in the end.'

'That will not happen,' said Alan fervently.

'Of course not,' said the old man. 'But if it does you need not worry. She'll never divorce you. Oh, no! And, of course, she herself will never give you the least, the very least, grounds for — not divorce, of course — but even uneasiness.'

'And how much', said Alan, 'how much is this wonderful mixture?'

'It is not so dear,' said the old man, 'as the spot-remover, as I think we agreed to call it. No. That is five thousand dollars; never a penny less. One has to be older than you to indulge in that sort of thing. One has to save up for it.'

'But the love-potion?' said Alan.

'Oh, that,' said the old man, opening the drawer in the kitchen table and taking out a tiny, rather dirty-looking phial. 'That is just a dollar.'

'I can't tell you how grateful I am,' said Alan, watching him fill it.

'I like to oblige,' said the old man. 'Then customers come back, later in life, when they are rather better-off, and want more expensive things. Here you are. You will find it very effective.'

'Thank you again,' said Alan. 'Goodbye.'

'*Au revoir*,' said the old man. 'Until we meet again.'

The Laugher

Heinrich Böll

Translated by Leila Vennewitz from the German

Heinrich Böll was born in 1917 in Cologne. The terrors he witnessed during his youth in Nazi Germany influenced much of his writing. His sense of moral outrage was often expressed through satire. His humour is that of the clown — bitter and sad. He was awarded the Nobel Prize for Literature in 1972.

When someone asks me what business I am in, I am seized with embarrassment: I blush and stammer, I who am otherwise known as a man of poise. I envy people who can say: I am a bricklayer. I envy barbers, bookkeepers, and writers the simplicity of their avowal, for all these professions speak for themselves and need no lengthy explanation, while I am constrained to reply to such questions: I am a laugher. An admission of this kind demands another, since I have to answer the second question: 'Is that how you make your living?' truthfully with 'Yes.' I actually do make a living at my laughing, and a good one too, for my laughing is — commercially speaking — much in demand. I am a good laugher, experienced, no one else laughs as well as I do, no one else has such command of the fine points of my art. For a long time, in order to avoid tiresome explanations, I called myself an actor, but my talents in the field of mime and elocution are so meager that I felt this designation to be too far from the truth: I love the truth, and the truth is: I am a laugher. I am neither a clown nor a comedian. I do not make people gay, I portray gaiety: I laugh like a Roman emperor, or like a sensitive schoolboy, I am as much at home in the laughter of the seventeenth century as in that of the nineteenth, and when occasion demands I laugh my way through the centuries, all classes of society, all categories of age: it is simply a skill which I have acquired, like the skill of being able to repair shoes. In my breast I harbor the laughter of America, the laughter of Africa, white, red, yellow laughter — and for the right fee I let it peal out in accordance with the director's requirements.

I have become indispensable; I laugh on records, I laugh on tape, and television directors treat me with respect. I laugh mournfully, moderately, hysterically; I laugh like a streetcar conductor or like an apprentice in the grocery business; laughter in the morning, laughter in the evening, nocturnal laughter, and the laughter of twilight. In short: wherever and however laughter is required — I do it.

It need hardly be pointed out that a profession of this kind is tiring, especially as I have also — this is my specialty — mastered the art of infectious laughter; this has also made me indispensable to third- and fourth-rate comedians, who are scared — and with good reason — that their audiences will miss their punchlines, so I spend most evenings in nightclubs as a kind of discreet claque, my job being to laugh infectiously during the weaker parts of the program. It has to be carefully timed: my hearty, boisterous laughter must not come too soon, but neither must it come too late, it must come just at the right spot: at the prearranged moment I burst out laughing, the whole audience roars with me, and the joke is saved.

But as for me, I drag myself exhausted to the checkroom, put on my overcoat, happy that I can go off duty at last. At home I usually find telegrams waiting for me: 'Urgently require your laughter. Recording Tuesday,' and a few hours later I am sitting in an overheated express train bemoaning my fate.

I need scarcely say that when I am off duty or on vacation I have little inclination to laugh: the cowhand is glad when he can forget the cow, the bricklayer when he can forget the mortar, and carpenters usually have doors at home which don't work or drawers which are hard to open. Confectioners like sour pickles, butchers like marzipan, and the baker prefers sausage to bread; bullfighters raise pigeons for a hobby, boxers turn pale when their children have nosebleeds: I find all this quite natural, for I never laugh off duty. I am a very solemn person, and people consider me — perhaps rightly so — a pessimist.

During the first years of our married life, my wife would often say to me: 'Do laugh!' but since then she has come to realize that I cannot grant her this wish. I am happy when I am free to relax my tense face muscles, my frayed spirit, in profound solemnity. Indeed, even other people's laughter gets on my nerves, since it reminds me too much of my profession. So our marriage is a quiet, peaceful one, because my wife has also forgotten how to laugh: now and again I catch her smiling, and I smile too. We converse in low tones, for I detest the noise of the nightclubs, the noise that sometimes fills the recording studios. People who do not know me think I am taciturn. Perhaps I am, because I have to open my mouth so often to laugh.

I go through life with an impassive expression, from time to time permitting myself a gentle smile, and I often wonder whether I have ever laughed. I think not. My brothers and sisters have always known me for a serious boy.

So I laugh in many different ways, but my own laughter I have never heard.

The Last Days

of a

Famous Mime

Peter Carey

Peter Carey was born in 1943 in rural Victoria. His first collection of short stories *The Fat Man in History* was pubished in 1974. In his stories surrealism and realism blend to create a nightmarish world, both fantastic and real. His characters are often social failures. Carey's macabre humour underlies his strong sense of the absurd. His later novels *Bliss* and *Oscar and Lucinda* have been highly acclaimed.

1

The Mime arrived on Alitalia with very little luggage: a brown paper parcel and what looked like a woman's handbag.

Asked the contents of the brown paper parcel he said, 'String.'

Asked what the string was for he replied: 'Tying up bigger parcels.'

It had not been intended as a joke, but the Mime was pleased when the reporters laughed. Inducing laughter was not his forte. He was famous for terror.

Although his state of despair was famous throughout Europe, few guessed at his hope for the future. 'The string,' he explained, 'is a prayer that I am always praying.'

Reluctantly he untied his parcel and showed them the string. It was blue and when extended measured exactly fifty-three meters.

The Mime and the string appeared on the front pages of the evening papers.

2

The first audiences panicked easily. They had not been prepared for his ability to mime terror. They fled their seats continually. Only to return again.

Like snorkel divers they appeared at the doors outside the concert hall with red faces and were puzzled to find the world as they had left it.

3

Books had been written about him. He was the subject of an award-winning film. But in his first morning in a provincial town he was distressed to find that his performance had not been liked by the one newspaper's one critic.

'I cannot see,' the critic wrote, 'the use of invoking terror in an audience.'

The Mime sat on his bed, pondering ways to make his performance more light-hearted.

4

As usual he attracted women who wished to still the raging storms of his heart. They attended his bed like highly paid surgeons operating on a difficult case. They were both passionate and intelligent. They did not suffer defeat lightly.

5

Wrongly accused of merely miming love in his private life he was somewhat surprised to be confronted with hatred.

'Surely,' he said, 'if you now hate me, it was you who were imitating love, not I.'

'You always were a slimy bastard,' she said. 'What's in that parcel?'

'I told you before,' he said helplessly, 'string.'

'You're a liar,' she said.

But later when he untied the parcel he found that she had opened it to check on his story. Her understanding of the string had been perfect. She had cut it into small pieces like spaghetti in a lousy restaurant.

6

Against the advice of the tour organizers he devoted two concerts entirely to love and laughter. They were disasters. It was felt that love and laughter were not, in his case, as instructive as terror.

The next performance was quickly announced.

TWO HOURS OF REGRET

Tickets sold quickly. He began with a brief interpretation of love using it merely as a prelude to regret which he elaborated on in a complex and moving performance which left the audience pale and shaken. In a final flourish he passed from regret to loneliness to terror. The audience devoured the terror like brave tourists eating the hottest curry in an Indian restaurant.

7

'What you are doing,' she said, 'is capitalizing on your neuroses. Personally I find it disgusting, like someone exhibiting their clubfoot, or Turkish beggars with strange deformities.'

He said nothing. He was mildly annoyed at her presumption: that he had not thought this many, many times before.

With perfect misunderstanding she interpreted his passivity as disdain.

Wishing to hurt him, she slapped his face.

Wishing to hurt her, he smiled brilliantly.

8

The story of the blue string touched the public imagination. Small brown paper packages were sold at the door of his concert.

Standing on stage he could hear the packages being noisily unwrapped. He thought of American matrons buying Muslim prayer rugs.

9

Exhausted and weakened by the heavy schedule he fell prey to the doubts that had pricked at him insistently for years. He lost all sense of direction and spent many listless hours by himself, sitting in a motel room listening to the air conditioner.

He had lost confidence in the social uses of controlled terror. He no longer understood the audience's need to experience the very things he so desperately wished to escape from.

He emptied the ashtrays fastidiously.

He opened his brown paper parcel and threw the small pieces of string down the cistern. When the torrent of white water subsided they remained floating there like flotsam from a disaster at sea.

10

The Mime called a press conference to announce that there would be no more concerts. He seemed small and foreign and smelt of garlic. The press regarded him without enthusiasm. He watched their hovering pens anxiously, unsuccessfully willing them to write down his words.

Briefly he announced that he wished to throw his talent open to broader influences. His skills would be at the disposal of the people, who would be free to request his services for any purpose at any time.

His skin seemed sallow but his eyes seemed as bright as those on a nodding fur mascot on the back window ledge of an American car.

11

Asked to describe death he busied himself taking Polaroid photographs of his questioners.

12

Asked to describe marriage he handed out small cheap mirrors with MADE IN TUNISIA written on the back.

13

His popularity declined. It was felt that he had become obscure and beyond the understanding of ordinary people. In response he requested easier questions. He held back nothing of himself in his effort to please his audience.

14

Asked to describe an airplane he flew three times around the city, only injuring himself slightly on landing.

15

Asked to describe a river, he drowned himself.

16

It is unfortunate that this, his last and least typical performance, is the only one which has been recorded on film.

There is a small crowd by the riverbank, no more than thirty people. A small, neat man dressed in a gray suit picks his way through some children who seem more interested in the large plastic toy dog they are playing with.

He steps into the river, which, at the bank, is already quite deep. His head is only visible above the water for a second or two. And then he is gone.

A policeman looks expectantly over the edge, as if waiting for him to reappear. Then the film stops.

Watching this last performance it is difficult to imagine how this man stirred such emotions in the hearts of those who saw him.

The Chaser   *John Collier*

Discussion

1   Why does the old man say 'Au revoir' at the end of this short short story? What is implied by this remark?

2   'That is love!' cried Alan when the old man explained the effects of the love potion. Was he right? Give reasons for your point of view.

3   A *euphemism* is a mild or vague expression used in place of a harsh, vulgar or socially unacceptable one. What euphemisms are used in 'The Chaser', and how do they add to the effectiveness of the story?

Activities

1   Imagine that during dinner, on the night after his visit to Pell Street, Alan slipped some drops of the love potion into Diana's drink. Diana was being particularly nasty to him that evening. Write a page to show something of Diana's original mood, followed by the change brought about by the potion.

2   Write a page describing Alan's second visit to the old man.

3 People often wish to change themselves. They are not satisfied, maybe, with their abilities, their intelligence or their looks. Imagine one of the following situations, and write a story of your own based around the idea.

- A potion is invented which, when swallowed, prevents people from ageing.
- People are able, through plastic surgery, to be turned into complete physical replicas of their heroes or heroines.
- The government offers parents, on the birth of each child, a Free Conditioning Program. Parents may choose whether they wish their children to have the Business Sense Course, the Social Success Course, or the Artistic Talent Course. All children must undergo one of these courses. Parents who avoid this offer are hunted down by the paramilitary police.

The Laugher *Heinrich Böll*

Discussion

1 Is this story funny, sad or both? Give reasons for your point of view.

2 What do you think are some of the ideas about human behaviour that we are asked to consider in this short short story? Discuss three of them.

3 What do you imagine is implied by the label 'confessional' when applied to literature? Do you think this story might be termed 'confessional'? What are the qualities, do you suppose, of confessional writing?

Activities

1 Describe, in half a page, a significant moment from a working day in the life of The Laugher. Next, also in half a page, describe a moment of relaxation as he and his wife share an enjoyable night out.

2 In a page, write a short short story to describe the confessions of 'The Cryer'.

3 On film sets, stunt men and women often are employed to behave in specific ways. Some fight with swords; some are professional fallers. Other are good at portraying panic in crowd scenes, or merely acting as dead bodies. Some lend their hands, hair or legs for close-up scenes, and the rest of them is never seen on camera. This is not realistic human behaviour. Write a story about one such stunt actor. Add some natual human behaviour such as pride, jealousy or revenge, and see if you can create an interesting story from the mixture.

The Last Days of a Famous Mime   *Peter Carey*

Discussion

1   What sort of a person is the famous mime? Does he change during the course of the story?

2   What do you think 'The Last Days of a Famous Mime' is about? What are some of the ideas present in this highly original piece of storytelling? How many ideas occurred to you as you read it?

3   **a**   What is meant by the *climax* of a story? Is there a climax to this story, and, if so, where does it occur?
    b   Does a story always need a climax? Explain.

Activities

1   On your own, devise and present a mime along the lines of the one referred to in section 6. Start by miming a love affair, then show how the affair ends and your character experiences regret, then loneliness, and, finally, terror.

2   Reread section 4 of Carey's story. It is a general summary of events. Rewrite this section in your own words, converting the general into the particular. Add detail, description and dialogue to bring the scene to life in a page of writing.

3   This short short story is told in sixteen separate sections. They move along erratically, jumping from one scene to the next like an old black-and-white movie. There is a surreal atmosphere to the story.
    Try writing a story of your own using Peter Carey's approach. Divide your story up into a series of short scenes. Choose your details carefully. Here are three suggestions.
    •   Put together a series of scenes from your own childhood.
    •   Record in slow motion an important incident from your life.
    •   Take a story from the newspapers, and tell it in a series of short episodes.

Phantom
at the Head
of the Table

Louis Allegri

The woman was playing some delicate Debussy on the piano. The man sitting on the sofa in the elegantly furnished drawing-room reflected that the scene was all a man could wish for.

Perfect. No! He drew his breath in sharply. He mustn't use that word — it always caused murderous feelings to erupt inside him.

As if he could murder a ghost!

But a spectre did loom over everything in that house, forming an invisible barrier between him and his fiancée, the girl at the piano, whose graceful beauty still retained much of the warm, trusting innocence of childhood. They were to be married in a few months, but the thought of that other man — the presence — sent a chill through him. How do you destroy a ghost?

She suddenly stopped playing with a massive discord and then stood up. 'I'm hopeless.'

'Hopeless? Why do you always demean yourself?' He walked over and put an arm about her shoulders. 'I thought it was per ... quite marvellous, Esther.'

'Poor Des,' she smiled. 'It was rubbish — when you've been used to hearing real talent.'

'Well, I liked it!'

She looked up at him. 'My dear, kind Desmond. You'd say the same thing if I played it backwards. You don't understand, I mean —'

'You mean I'm too insensitive to appreciate the difference, not like — ?'

'Let's not talk about Arnie — tonight of all nights. It's our wedding anniversary.' She turned away, shoulders bowed.

'You don't normally let me forget your perfect Adonis of a husband. He's everywhere in this place.'

He looked around and his gaze came to rest on the large painting over the marble fireplace. It showed a handsome, smiling man whose dark eyes always seemed to peer all round the room.

'Yes, he was a paragon of all that's talented and wonderful. And me? I'm not fit to lace his elegant shoes. And there are actually some of those still around. It's like some crazy fetish.'

'Don't. Please don't.' She walked across the room to stare out of the French windows on to a rain-swept, walled garden.

'Give me more time, Des,' she whispered. 'We were — so close. As if he were part of me. My whole reason for living rested on poor Arnie. I love you, Des,' she turned, a tear sparkling on her pale cheek, 'but no one can truly take his place. You know, Des,' she wiped the tear away, 'he really was like a Greek god. He could have had any woman he wanted. Yet he chose me. Six wonderful years we had together in complete harmony and trust.'

'Roses all the way,' he winced. 'Can't compete with that.' He glanced at the bunch of flowers he had brought, which lay, still wrapped on the table.

'Anything Arnie put his hands to turned to gold,' she said as though she hadn't heard him. 'Music, painting, everything. Did you know that is his own self-portrait?' She looked up at his picture. 'Arnie was the only man I'd ever loved — apart from Dad, of course. He was quite a wonderful man. Oh, and I'm not forgetting my dear, kind Des.' She hurried back to him and kissed him, her eyes filled with tears.

'I feel like a second-class intruder in this house,' he mumbled, looking at the sheen of her auburn hair, 'with a ghost at the head of the table.'

'Don't say such things.' Her voice was muffled. 'It — it's not nice.'

'Why? Do you think he's watching, surveying the crude interloper in his earthly paradise? The man's dead. He's no more. Why won't you accept that, Esther?'

'No!' she shook her head. 'Part of Arnie, at least, is still with me. I can still hear and feel his presence. Such a vital, conscious being like Arnie doesn't just disappear into nothing. He can't … *can't.*'

Almost overwhelmed by her vehemence, he pushed her gently away.

'I think I had better leave now, Esther. It's all a bit too much for me. I've done a few things in my time and am certainly far from perfect. Tonight is a night for you to commune with the gods. I'll leave you with your — your spirit of things past.' He hesitated before the melancholy in her grey eyes. 'I'll try to get here tomorrow night.'

Then anger suddenly replaced conciliation. 'I feel murder inside me for that — phantom. It's destroying you, Esther. He's been gone eight months now! He's a dead man rotting below ground. God, it's not right!'

'Stop … stop it!' She covered her ears. 'Please go now,' and she ran from the room.

He had to do it — for her sake. From his pocket he took the love letter that left so little to the imagination from — Elizabeth to Arnie. His whole body trembled in an ache of uncertainty, but then, in desperation, he walked swiftly to the bureau and with a shaking hand, slipped the letter at the back before hurrying out to his car in the drive.

The following night, he drove beneath a stony, grey sky towards her place hating himself. How could he have done such a thing, to have forged such a letter … from no one to no one. But, he couldn't let the dead control the living.

Then his mood changed. By God there would be a lot going for them both once that ghost had been destroyed completely.

He entered the house and walked into the drawing-room. The bureau was open, the letter gone. She must be upstairs.

But then he saw his fraudulent letter on a table. And there was also one from her to himself … and beside it an empty sleeping tablet bottle.

'Found this letter! Wouldn't believe it! But then — God, I remembered Elizabeth Thraxton — one of our friends! So much hate I felt it wasn't me … Poor Des. I'm not worth all that worrying. That woman's destroyed me now. Can't go on with this terrible wasteland in my head.'

'Esther!' he yelled, running out of the room and up the stairs. But he knew what he would find. That empty bottle beside the letter told the story.

The man standing at the top of the stairs said he was the police. 'You must be Desmond? Oh, she's all right. Got her to hospital in time.'

'Thank God!' He choked. 'How long will they keep her? When can we get her home?'

'Home? She is being charged with the murder of a Miss Thraxton. Miss Elizabeth Thraxton …'

The Well-bred Thief

Elizabeth Jolley

Elizabeth Jolley was born in Birmingham, England, in 1923, and came to Western Australia with her husband and three children in 1959. She was a nurse, salesperson and flying domestic before emerging as a significant contemporary writer. Jolley writes about eccentric characters, imbuing her stories with comic detail and moral good sense.

Roadside Mail 1,
Meduhla, W.A.
1 January

Dear Barbara,
You'll be surprised to have a letter from me. It's years since we moved up together from Fraser Street Mixed Infants and passed out from St Mary's Big Girls.

I had a mattock head sent from England and there in one of the newspapers used for packing was your picture! I suppose it's your husband with you and your son who has done so well at school.

You've hardly changed; well of course you're older, but you don't look any too old.

I'm sending you the manuscript of a book I've written. Please could you submit it for me? I notice you work for a publisher. I'm living all alone in the country waiting for the jarrah to grow. Donald and Mary have left home and there's no one to talk to except the fowls, that's why I've written this book.

No one at all knows I have written it. I have put in a postal order for expenses and a tea-cloth decorated with Kangaroo Paws. They are wild flowers, our National Emblem. They look better with the sun shining through the red and green plush of their stalks.

I suppose Peter will be going to University after getting such high marks. You must be proud of him.

This summer is very dry, all life seems withdrawn in this heat. The honey trees are covered in creamy balls of flower and the noise of the bees is like distant church music. These trees light up the countryside; they remind me of the candles of the horsechestnuts in England, though if I could see them again, I would know they are not at all like our honey trees.

I hope your winter is not too severe with fog and snow.

Very best wishes,
Mabel Morgan

Holly House,
Tarbridge,
Kent, U.K.
3 March

Dear Neckless,
I simply can't think of you by any other name than your old nickname. I have read your charming and poetical book. I am sure you can write, but the Question *is* What! *I found myself completely absorbed. I have let my impressions simmer, and have since had it read by one of the Younger Set at Trotter and Trotter. The Reader said* Perfectly True *things, but was absolutely* Not in Tune *with your writing, though you do have a* Taut and Telling *line. Your characters are very real, but would people want to read about the very real? You do rather overdo Beethoven. I am sure he is completely* Out *now. Years ago* we *discovered him. I remember my own elephantine gyrations to the grand finale of his Seventh. But do people* really *want Beethoven now? All this* maddens *me. You have a remarkable aptitude for evoking sights and sounds and especially smells. Why is the main character, Edna, so battered in the first half of the book, when in the second half she does all the battering? Leila certainly pulls the book into shape, as do the bulldozers in the new shopping centre — a clever image! I love your disastrous dinner party and the arrival of the police. You certainly understand the problems of teenage boys. Walter made my heart* bleed. *But why keep his box a secret? and why keep the reader in suspense over the killing of the little girl?*

Peter hopes to spend summer in Athens and will be starting University after the long vac. If he doesn't work for his exams we have threatened him with Australia. How on earth do you manage for culture *over there?*

Yours ever,
Barbara

Ps. What is jarrah? and why do you have to wait for it?

Roadside Mail 1,
Meduhla, W.A.
20 May

Dear Barbara,
I have just received your long letter of 3rd March. You forgot to put any stamps on it so it has come surface mail. I'm very relieved to have it at last. I'm interested in what you have to say about my book. In the writing I'm trying to discover if a person finds peace within himself rather than in the world outside or whether the true meaning of life really comes from external circumstances. Edna changes because she chooses the man with prospects rather than the man she loves. The second half of the book deals with her striving to rebuild her collapsed life. I have tried to show this unpleasant character as an honest one.

Leila and her mother are symbols of suburban comfort and complacency. For them there is no struggle, they don't know unemployment and poverty. For them there are no wars and no famines. In their lives there is no poetry or music either, and no drama of love and hate. Even the word 'government' really means nothing to them.

Walter, the product of Edna's unhappiness, does understand, but is inarticulate. He breaks away from the conventional education Edna wants for him, but later struggles back to the desirable comfort of the suburb. The girl from the greengrocery store is merely his accomplice. Neither of them can expect a wider horizon. The delayed explanations are necessary: if I revealed the contents of Walter's box too soon, there would be no point in the book.

I did not mean to write for a particular audience. I thought there might be many kinds of minds in the reading public. I realise you can't submit a second time to the same publisher, especially as you work there. I would be grateful if you would try another publisher please.

I hope you all keep well. I hope Peter studies as you want him to. It's no use for a young man to come out to Australia unless he has qualifications of some kind.

My best wishes to you,
Mabel

Ps. Jarrah is a kind of tree. I sold the farm, but am still living here as the new owner agreed to my staying on till my crop matured. I planted a jarrah forest. I'll be here for some time. The children have gone, as I told you. I do miss them.

Holly House,
Tarbridge,
Kent, U.K.
30 May

Dear Neckless,
I am appalled my letter went without a stamp. I do hope you didn't have to pay up. From March to May is rather a long time to wait for a letter. Really I am terribly sorry.

Life has been very erratic and hectic ever since Christmas and we all had colds and 'flu. Really our English winters! I will get out your manuscript again when I re-read your letter. At present we are trying to decide on fresh colour schemes for the hall and the bathroom. Matching towels are such a problem aren't they!

I wonder if you could do something for me? A friend has just emigrated to Sydney, her name is Mrs Flint, and the address is Avon Park. Do you think you could call on her? Thanks most awfully.

Yours,
Barbara

Roadside Mail 1,
Meduhla, W.A.
14 June

Dear Barbara,
Please don't worry about the unstamped letter. I never see the postman: he leaves the letters in a drum down on the road. It's too far for him to come up to the house.

I hope you are all better now.

I'd like to visit your friend Mrs Flint, but I don't think I'm able to go the two thousand miles over to Sydney. You see I only get up to town here about twice a year. I hope the lady is settling down; it takes a while to get used to a strange place. There is nothing worse than loneliness.

I'm looking forward to hearing from you soon.

Yours ever,
Mabel

As from Tarbridge,
Kent, U.K.
28 June

Dear Neckless,

I am being very wicked and stealing an airgraph from the firm. I did buy
one, but left it at home. I bring sandwiches to the office and type in the lunch
hour as my evenings are all filled up with meetings —

I am dreadfully ashamed, but I have to confess that for the moment I
have mislaid your book. How I can have lost it I can't imagine! I'm quite certain it's the first time in thirty-five years of handling manuscripts. You probably gathered I was in complete chaos when I wrote before. Peter had just collapsed with 'flu, Ernest went down while on a Business Trip and, though I
was sub-clinical, I got the <u>Full After-effects</u>. I pushed everything into the
spare room. Then, when your letter came I was <u>Absolutely Appalled</u> that the
manuscript wasn't where I thought it was. I'm quite sure it will turn up. I'm
one of those people who find things if they don't look for them.

I'm not being casual about this. I realise apologies won't help! I'm inclined
to advise you to wait a little before submitting the book anywhere else.

Of course its '<u>Not Done</u>' for me to quote what other Readers have said.
But Edna's squalid life alone in the hut certainly impressed and so did the
poignant luxury life of the white and gold bedroom scenes later. Ah! the sad-
ness of loving too late … And, added to all this, your apparent knowledge of
life inside a prison. However could you give the appearance of being so familiar with this?

Ah well, I hope you will be forgiving about the loss of Edna and Leila
and all of them.

I am not so chaotic as a rule. If you can stand the expense and my
<u>Outspokenness</u>, I'll be only too glad to read anything else you care to send.

Yours ever,
Barbara

Ps. I feel awful.

Roadside Mail 1,
Meduhla, W.A.
6 July

Dear Barbara,
Thank you for the letter. I was so impatient to read it, I opened it right down there on the road. I must admit it is a terrible shock to me that the book is lost. An unbearable loneliness on top of the loneliness I've got already came over me as I read your letter. I felt as if I'd lost a child somewhere and was too far away, too isolated, to do anything about it. I came straight back up to the house. It's intolerable here, there's no one I can talk to about the loss of the book. I keep walking on to the verandah and looking down the long paddock. But there's nothing there except the tufted grass all the way to the edge of the bush. It's so quiet except for the noise of the crows. Their indifference only makes the loneliness worse. I feel quite helpless so far away from the places where I could enquire and search for my book. I have never felt like this before. It's as if I can't really believe what you have written, and yet I know I must believe it. I'm sorry to go on like this!

I should not have troubled you with it when you have such a busy life.

Please do write at once when you find it. Perhaps by now you will have found it. I do hope so.

Yours ever,
Mabel

Roadside Mail 1,
Meduhla, W.A.
20 October

Dear Barbara,
It's nearly the end of October and I've been waiting since July hoping for a letter from you. Have you by any chance found the manuscript of my book *The Leila Family*? I do hope you have.

I hope you are all well and that Peter will enjoy University.

It's very dry and dusty here. I seem to spend my days going down to wait for the mail and watching the sky for rain clouds. Please write soon.

Yours ever,
Mabel

Holly House,
Tarbridge,
Kent, U.K.
10 November

Dear Neckless,

I am ashamed and quite <u>appalled</u> by your letter. I can't believe all those months have gone by and all the time you have been waiting for your manu-script to come safely back home. It's unthinkable — you alone in your little wooden hut under the hot sun with your galvanised water-tanks running dry — is this a correct picture I have?

I have been in the throes of an <u>occasion</u> since our correspondence. Please don't argue, I insist on sending you ten pounds towards making up for the loss of the manuscript. I insist that you accept it. I shall not <u>feel</u> the sending of it, as I am about to receive a Bonus for something I am doing at Trotter and Trotter. I am afraid the manuscript did not turn up during our spring-clean-ing and it's too late to enquire at the railway now —

I've had your name at the top of my list. I wish I had got my letter in first. I am sorry.

Yours,
Barbara

Ps. In August we had 10 days motoring in the Pyrenees. Glorious weather.

Roadside Mail 1,
Meduhla, W.A.
18 November

Dear Barbara,
Please don't upset yourself so much and please don't send me the money. As Autolycus says in 'A Winter's Tale', 'Simply the thing I am shall make me live.'

I can't help hoping the book will be found.

Yes, you are right, we have water-tanks, but not dry yet thank good-ness. The home is weatherboard with a verandah all round. We have an iron roof and the tanks are to one side. I have roses and geraniums and of course the jarrah saplings, what's left of them, after Donald and his friend made a dirt track of the place with their old cars.

Donald and Mary are still away somewhere. I do miss them. I keep hoping for them to come. And I do hope the book will be found.

I hope all is well with your family.

Yours,
Mabel

Holly House,
Tarbridge,
Kent, U.K.
28 November

Dear Neckless,
We didn't do 'Winter's Tale' at school. How come you know it? I wouldn't have thought Shakespeare had got down under!

I was glad to get your letter and to know you can take things so philo-sophically. I am also glad to lower my sights over the manuscript, but I do want to send you <u>something</u> and have done so today. I have posted you a dress length. Please don't feel I have been extravagant, it's something I happened to have by me. I hope it will not be ruined crossing the equator. The psychedelic colours are just not <u>me</u>. I hope they will be <u>you</u>. I expect you have long evenings to fill up, so have enclosed two adult education essays I have written. You may enjoy reading them, also Mrs Coles notes on Poe.

I would be very interested to know if you are thinking of writing more about Leila and Edna and the others. If you are perhaps you could write back at once. Quick notes will do, and send me any other ideas you have. Perhaps you could do this soon, as soon as possible please. Could you?

Peter is thrilled with his campus. His digs are rather far off, but he seems to have good food.

Yours,
Barbara

Ps. My parcel won't get to you in time for Christmas, but it should be there soon after.
Pps. You are sure aren't you that no one else knows that you have written the book?

Lost

For Words

Richard Baines

Richard Baines was born in the north of England in 1941. He hitch-hiked
to Australia, after spending 4 years teaching in Uganda and Kenya. He is the
co-author of several English textbooks.

Jenny came running down the aisle. Her dark hair was swinging wildly.
This time the book I held in my hand had a red cover.

'Another one?' she cried, her eyes shining.

I love it when she does that. Her eyes are a deep brown, and her
lashes are long with a little curl on them. I still feel excited when I see
her, though now I also feel sad for I know our relationship is over.

It began almost the first day I came to the shop. It's a small shop,
and there were only the two of us working there, apart from the owner,
Mr Bishop, and he usually kept himself locked away in his office. So we
had the place to ourselves you might say. We had our first kiss by the

Penguin Classics, tucked away in the corner. We put the classics down there because no one reads them, though by the end of our first fortnight I was getting to know them pretty well. Jenny seemed to have taken to me, and I was mad about her of course and getting more involved every day.

'This is Paul,' Mr Bishop had said when I turned up for work that first morning. 'Be a good girl, Jenny. Show him the ropes.'

She certainly had.

And then an unexpected thing happened. She switched off. There's no other way of describing it: she just switched off. She never really gave me a reason. She calmly said she thought we should put a stop to it, and just as I was getting up the courage to invite her to spend the night at my flat! I felt terrible, I can tell you, and I tried to explain how frustrating the whole experience had been and she just smiled at me with those beautiful deep brown eyes and we had our first and last row.

Just opposite Biography.

That was many months ago, of course. I'm all right now. I keep thinking back to it, however, whenever I see her all worked up and excited. I just wish I could persuade myself that she hadn't done the whole thing on purpose.

'It's another Christie.'

She took the book, which had a picture of a serious-minded man looking out of a window on its bright red cover, and opened it.

'It's the same as the others.'

She turned to the back, and sure enough, there by the inside binding was a ragged edge where the last four pages had been torn out. Torn straight out. Someone had carefully placed a finger on the top inside of the book and slowly removed the final four pages of an Agatha Christie murder story.

What sort of person would do that?

'It's those students from the High School,' said Jenny.

Just like them, I thought. They don't like reading and it's the sort of thing they would find funny — tearing back pages out of detective stories so readers would never be able to find out who did it! I must confess I smiled when I thought of that.

I didn't smile for long though, for I could hear the office door behind me open and Mr Bishop come out. The office is at the front, next to New Releases and TV Tie-Ins. Mr Bishop has a long face, and looks a bit like a moose with specs on. He always wears a suit, even on very hot days. He's a good boss. I can't say I like him or dislike him really, but I've done a bit of thinking and decided that I don't want to stay in a bookshop all my life, so I've been working hard lately. I've sold a lot of books. I'm good at it.

Jenny's not so keen. She's quite happy stocking the shelves, drinking coffee or having a bit of a chat about the people in the town. Or her family. It's funny about Jenny's family. She talks about all of them but her dad. She really hates her dad. She never says anything, but I can tell.

'What is it this time?' said Mr Bishop. 'Another detective story?'

We have a pile of them in the back room. There are twelve of them there. This is the thirteenth. All with the last few pages torn out.

'Yes,' I said. 'It's *The Murder of Roger Ackroyd*.'

'Mrs Price was in here the other day. You know. That white-haired old lady from the Retirement Village. She spends hours browsing and never buys anything. Shouldn't be surprised if it's her. They shouldn't come in and browse if they don't intend to buy.'

I should have mentioned it: Mr Bishop is a real Scrooge. I know about Scrooge now since my time in Classics. Mr Bishop wouldn't spend anything he didn't need to. I've often wondered why he employed both Jenny and myself, but I suppose he thought it would be good for business. Well, it has been in a way. We're doing well.

'She discovered the first one, didn't she? It's bound to be her.'

I couldn't see it myself. Why would an old lady hand in a book if she'd just vandalised it? Another thing struck me as odd about Mr bishop when he said that: he didn't seem angry. Not even upset. His next remark was weird too.

'She talks, you know, old Mrs Price. We can't afford that sort of publicity around the town. It'll destroy us.'

I took *Roger Ackroyd* into the back room and put him with the others. If this went on much longer the Crime shelves would soon be empty, and we did good business in Crime. When I returned to the shop Mr Bishop was still standing there with Jenny. She winked at me as she went back to dusting the coffee table books on the centre stand.

Have I mentioned her eyes?

Mr Bishop looked pensive. His brow furrows up into several wavy lines when he does that. I remember it distinctly at about number nine. We had just lost the last chapter of one of those mediaeval detective stories. 'If this goes on,' he said, 'I shall have to cut down on my staff, I'm afraid.' He had that same look now, pensive but not angry.

'She was in here yesterday afternoon.' He turned and went back to his office.

It's true, Mrs Price had been in yesterday afternoon. But it was also true that the *Roger Ackroyd* book had been complete when we closed the shop. I'd checked them all on that shelf before I'd left.

So it had to be one of us.

That set me thinking. Why would any one of us want to tear up our own books? It all seemed so pointless. I mean what could possibly be the

Phantom at the Head of the Table   *Louis Allegri*

Discussion

1   How many murders were committed in this story. Who murdered whom?

2   What sort of relationship do you think Esther had with her father? What effect did this have upon her later relationships with men?

3   Sometimes a story depends upon the choice of a *key word* to make it work. Examine the importance of the word 'perfect' in Allegri's short short story, and discuss how central it is to the working of the piece.

Activities

1   'Home? She is being charged with the murder of a Miss Thraxton. Miss Elizabeth Thraxton ...' — What happens next? Write half a page.

2   Was Arnie perfect? Describe a breakfast scene one morning between Esther and Arnie. In your page of writing, make use of some of the details referred to in the original story.

3   Murder stories are hard to write. There must be a motive for the killing. If possible, the ending should not be predictable. The plot is very important and must be carefully worked out beforehand. You can find some good ideas for murder stories in the tabloid newspapers. If you would like some other starting points, here are three.
   • One identical twin is jealous of another ...
   • A highly intelligent university professor plans the perfect murder ...
   • A hired killer accidentally murders the wrong woman ...

The Well-bred Thief   *Elizabeth Jolley*

Discussion

1   What happened in this story? How do you know?

2   Discuss the relationship between these two women. Would this have been the same if they had been next-door neighbours? Explain your point of view.

3   Look at Barbara's writing style. What does it tell us about her character? Give specific examples, (choice of words, underlinings, use of capital letters, sentence structure, etc.) when presenting your answer.

Activities

1   In pairs, prepare a reading of these letters, one student reading Mabel's letters and the other reading Barbara's. See if you can present the tone of

voice of each letter in your reading. The speed of your reading and the emphasis of individual words will help you achieve this.

2   Do you find 'The Well-bred Thief' sad or funny? Does it arouse other emotions in you? Discuss your responses in a page of writing.

3   Many writers have used this letter-writing form of story-telling. Elizabeth Jolley has done it on several occasions. Try this approach to the short short story yourself. Here are three suggestions. Write a story:
   • told entirely through letters or postcards
   • told through memo slips and formal messages
   • told through diary entries and computer printouts.

Lost for Words   *Richard Baines*

Discussion

1   Why does this story end the way it does? What was your reaction on first reading the ending?

2   Who do you think was responsible for the crime? Give your reasons for suspecting either Jenny, Paul or Mr Bishop of removing the final pages from the detective stories.

3   Notice how the *flashback* technique is used in this story. What is a 'flashback', and what are the advantages of using it in a story such as this?

Activities

1   What is the tone of voice of the speaker in this story? Read the piece aloud, revealing Paul's character through your presentation.

2   Imagine that Jenny decides to visit a psychiatrist. In a page of writing, record their conversation. Take what you have learned about her in 'Lost for Words' as the starting point for this conversation.

3   In 'Lost for Words', the reader is asked to be the detective and solve the crime. The problem with plots of this kind is that the short short story does not give the writer much time to set up motives and clues for a variety of suspects. It is a challenge. Try it for yourself. Start by deciding upon the crime. Here are three ideas to get you thinking.
   • Two school classrooms burn down one dark night.
   • A writer has his computer stolen. His next novel is in it.
   • A beautiful actress becomes ill the day before the opening night of a new show. Tests reveal food poisoning.
      Keep your story as simple as possible and limit your list of suspects to two or three. Provide each with a motive. Reveal the culprit in the last line.

APPENDIX I   Australian Short Short Story Project

Twelve of the stories in this anthology were written by Australian writers. Some of these authors are well-known, others are not. Some are professional writers, others are students still at school. All of the contributors are alive today. It might be interesting to make a special study of these pieces.

Birthday	Mary Roberts
Are You	Sarah Katherine Pidgeon
East Wind	Gillian Dawson
The Clearing	Martyn Hereward
The List of All Possible Answers	Peter Goldsworthy
The Pepper Tree	Wendy Stack
The Colonial Girl	Betty Roberts
A Deafening Silence	Vikki Goatham
The Parasite	Sarah O'Donnell
A Snake Down Under	Glenda Adams
The Last Days of a Famous Mime	Peter Carey
The Well-bred Thief	Elizabeth Jolley

1   Select six of the stories from the list above, and read them.

2   Name them at the top of your paper.

3   Write a 600-word essay discussing the stories you have read.

4   As you write you might like to consider some of the following:
   a   Are the stories noticeably Australian in content?
   b   Are they noticeably Australian in style?
   c   What, if anything, do they have in common?
   d   Do they throw light upon the way Australians live, act or think?
   e   Which stories do you like, and why? Which do you find less appealing, and why?

5   Finally, complete the essay by stating your conclusions after having read these six stories.

APPENDIX II   Guidelines for the Writer

One of the chief purposes of this book is to help students develop their own creative writing skills. Both 'Are You' and 'The Parasite' were written by students while still at school. While each writer will develop his or her own style and area of interest, it is still possible to outline a few general suggestions which may be helpful.

1 Generally a short short story only focuses on one thing. There is not the time to develop a full cast of characters, fashion a complex plot or unwind a lengthy storyline.

2 Cut down on all that action, and start concentrating on creating interesting characters, relationships and moods.

3 Give your stories detail.

4 In general, aim for a realistic balance between dialogue and narrative. Chop and change between dialogue and narrative. Some stories, of course, will not do this, but be aware of the choice.

5 Do not be satisfied with the first idea that comes into your mind. Work towards something more original.

6 Avoid clichés. Never use a simile or metaphor that you have heard before.

7 George Orwell suggested that a writer should not use a long word when a simple one will do. You might find this good advice.

8 Your stories must not be predictable. The reader should not be able to forsee what is coming.

9 Your stories must be believable.

10 Finally, remember that writing a story is a process. A piece of writing will probably have to go through several drafts and much alteration before it is finished.

APPENDIX III Story Checklist

For each of the short short stories collected in *Paper Windows*, the relevant Activity question number 3 suggests that the reader attempts to write a story of his or her own. There is a wide range of approaches suggested throughout the book, of course, and it might prove useful to list them here. Sometimes your choice of story might depend upon its style or technical approach rather than upon its subject matter or genre.

Allegory
- Write a tale in which life is presented as a rowing race, a game of blindman's buff, a jail sentence, a cricket match... (*The Falling Girl*, p. 140)

Detection
- Solve the problem of the classrooms which burnt down one dark night. (*Lost for Words*, p. 173)
- Solve the problem of the writer who had his computer stolen while his next novel was still in it. (*Lost for Words*, p. 173)
- Solve the problem of the beautiful actress who came down with food poisoning the day before her new show opened. (*Lost for Words*, p. 173)

Fantasy
- Write about a man who deliberately gives himself up to be eaten by a beautiful but dangerous flower. (*The Wife's Story*, p. 136)
- Show what happens when life becomes a frightening large-scale version of a popular television quiz game. (*The Wife's Story*, p. 136)

Ghost
- Write a story of a ghost who walks the earth protecting the life of the girl he once loved. (*The Return*, p. 94)
- Write a story in which a ghost, killed unjustly, is doomed to re-enact the event every year. There is only one way in which her soul can be laid to rest ... (*The Return*, p. 94)

Horror
- Show animals, birds and insects acting in unpredictable ways. (*The Fly*, p. 12)

Humour
- Write a horror story that fails to horrify. (*The Fly*, p. 12)
- Write a story starting with a line from a children's nursery rhyme or early reader. (*Fat Cat*, p. 63)

- Write a story in which a clumsy ghost has trouble controlling his supernatural powers. (*The Return*, p. 94)
- Write a story in which an adult behaves like a child, or someone behaves in an anti-social fashion. (*The List of All Possible Answers*, p. 66)

Love
- Write a story about an unexpected or unlikely love affair. (*Once In Love with Carla*, p. 35)

Murder
- Write a story in which one identical twin is jealous of another. (*Phantom at the Head of the Table*, p. 162)
- Write a story in which a highly intelligent university professor plans the perfect murder. (*Phantom at the Head of the Table*, p. 162)
- Write a story in which a hired killer accidentally murders the wrong woman. (*Phantom at the Head of the Table*, p. 162)

Mystery
- Examine a marriage where one partner has a guilty secret. (*Love Letter Straight from the Heart*, p. 32)

Personal
- Write a story in which a person experiences a moment of self-knowledge. (*The Pepper Tree*, p. 74)
- Write a story in which a person slowly regains consciousness. Where is he/she? What has happened? (*The Toy Girl*, p. 23)

Relationships
- Examine what happens when a young man and an older woman are thrown into each other's company. (*The Model*, p. 124)

Science fiction
- Write about a girl from the twenty-second century who suddenly finds herself in present-day Sydney. (*The Wife's Story*, p. 136)
- Explore what happens when people manage to change themselves physically. (*The Chaser*, p. 148)

Social
- Make the reader more aware of social problems. (*The Headache*, p. 81)
- Show how the fortunes of people change during the course of their lives. (*Spotlight*, p. 106)
- Write a story in which social attitudes and values have been turned around. (*Do You Want My Opinion?*, p. 116)

- Show how a stunt actor is trapped between real life and life in the movies. (*The Laugher*, p. 151)

Suspense
- Take an ordinary situation and turn it into something frightening. (*A Teacher's Rewards*, p. 2)

Technical
- Write a story where the first and last lines are given to you. (*Birthday*, p. 9)
- Write a story inspired by a particular line. (*The Grasshopper and the Bell Cricket*, p. 38)
- Introduce the reader to three separate worlds and then show how they connect. (*The Hairpiece*, p. 78)
- Re-tell a well-known story from a new angle. (*The Parasite*, p. 109)
- Tell a story in a series of short static scenes. (*A Snake Down Under*, p. 121, *The Last Days of a Famous Mime*, p. 154)
- Tell a story through letters and postcards. (*The Well-bred Thief*, p. 165)
- Tell a story through memo slips and formal messages. (*The Well-bred Thief*, p. 165)
- Tell a story through diary entries and computer printouts. (*The Well-bred Thief*, p. 165)

Youth
- Write a story about a teenage problem that concerns you. (*East Wind*, p. 25)
- Compose a typical teenage conversation. (*Through the Wilderness*, p. 60)
- Write a story about a child who leaves home at an early age. (*A Deafening Silence*, p. 102)

War
- Imagine someone 'presumed dead' who returns home after the war is over. (*Day to Remember*, p. 46)
- Write a war story set in the twentieth century in which not one shot is fired. (*The Clearing*, p. 49)
- Focus on an insignificant incident and use it to make an observation about war and the people caught up in it. (*Gregory*, p. 52)

APPENDIX IV Writing Techniques and devices

For each of the short short stories in *Paper Windows*, the relevant Discussion question number 3 is a language question. It asks about the writing techniques or devices used in the story. For anyone wishing to revise these writing techniques or devices the reading of the relevant short short story might prove helpful and entertaining.

Writing technique/Device	Short short story
Allusion	*Do You Want My Opinion?*, p. 116
Atmosphere	*Christmas Meeting*, p. 91
Cliché	*Examination Day*, p. 132
Climax	*The Last Days of a Famous Mime*, p. 154
Contrast	*Day to Remember*, p. 46
Detail	*Are You*, p. 20
Episodic writing	*A Snake Down Under*, p. 121
Euphemism	*The Chaser*, p. 148
Flashback	*Lost for Words*, p. 173
Foreshadowing	*The Headache*, p. 81
Imagery	*The Falling Girl*, p. 140
Irony	*The Hairpiece*, p. 78
Jargon	*Spotlight*, p. 106
Key word	*Phantom at the Head of the Table*, p. 162
Layout	*The List of All Possible Answers*, p. 66
Linking ends of story	*Birthday*, p. 9
Metaphor	*Gregory*, p. 52
Motif	*A Teacher's Rewards*, p. 2
Oxymoron	*A Deafening Silence*, p. 102
Plot	*The Return*, p. 94
Parody	*The List of All Possible Answers*, p. 66
Point of view	*The Clearing*, p. 49
Repetition	*The Grasshopper and the Bell Cricket*, p. 38
Satire	*Through the Wilderness*, p. 60
Sentence length	*The Wife's Story*, p. 136
Setting	*The Model*, p. 124
Simile	*Love Letters Straight from the Heart*, p. 32
Symbol	*The Pepper Tree*, p. 74
The Five Senses	*The Toy Girl*, p. 23
Theme	*Once in Love with Carla*, p. 35
Tone	*East Wind*, p. 25
Vocabulary	*The Parasite*, p. 109

Acknowlegements
The author would like to thank Connie de Silva for her valued guidance as editor, Jane Farago for proofreading and Marie Kelly for all her help and encouragement with this project. He would also like to thank the students of the Hills Grammar School for being the unwitting guineapigs for some of this material, as well as the witting proofreaders of all of it.

The author and publisher would like to thank the following organisations and sources for their assistance with respect to copyright material:

'Birthday' by Mary Roberts reprinted by permission of the author; 'The Fly' by Arthur Porges reprinted by permission of the author and the author's agents, Scott Meredith Literary Agency Inc., 845 Third Avenue, New York, New York 10022; 'Are You' by Sarah Katherine Pidgeon reprinted from *Midnight Dip*, edited by Catherine Hammond, Millennium Books, 1990: an imprint of E. J. Dwyer, Newtown, NSW 2042; 'The Toy Girl' © Paula Clark taken from *True to Life*, ed. Susan Hemmings — 1986. Reprinted with kind permission from Sheba Feminist Press; 'East Wind' by Gillian Dawson reprinted by permission of the author; 'The Grasshopper and the Bell Cricket' by Yasunari Kawabata reprinted by permission of Picador; 'Day to Remember' by James Clavell reprinted by permission of Foreign Rights Inc.; 'Through the Wilderness' by Michael Frayn reprinted from *On the Outskirts*, Collins 1964; 'The List of All Possible Answers' by Peter Goldsworthy from *Zooing* and 'A Snake Down Under' by Glenda Adams from *The Hottest Night of the Century*, reprinted by permission of Angus & Robertson, Sydney; 'The Pepper Tree' by Wendy Stack reprinted from *Kissing the Toad & other stories*, ed. Doug Macleod, Penguin Books Australia Ltd; 'The Headache' © Ann Hunter taken from *Everyday Matters*, ed. the Sheba Collective — 1982. Reprinted with kind permission from Sheba Feminist Press; 'The Colonial Girl' by Betty Roberts reprinted by permission of the author; 'A Deafening Silence' by Vikki Goatham reprinted by permission of the author; 'Do You Want My Opinion?' by ME Kerr reprinted from *Sixteen*, ed. Donald Gallo, HarperCollins Publishers Limited, 'The Model' by Bernard Malamud reprinted by permission of Russell & Volkening as agents for the author, Copyright 1983 by Bernard Malamud; 'The Falling Girl' by Dino Buzzati reprinted by permission of Arnoldo Mondadori Ltd; 'The Chaser' by John Collier reprinted by permission of the Peters Fraser & Dunlop Group Ltd; 'The Last Days of a Famous Mime' reprinted from *Exotic Pleasures* by Peter Carey published by University of Queensland Press, 1990; 'The Well-bred Thief' by Elizabeth Jolley first published in *South Pacific Stories*, ed. C & H Tifflin, Department of English, University of Queensland, St Lucia, 1980, pp122–312, © Elizabeth Jolley.